TIME AND THE RANI

DOCTOR WHO
TIME AND THE RANI

based on the BBC television series by Pip and Jane
Baker by arrangement with the British Broadcasting
Corporation

PIP AND JANE BAKER

Number 127 in the
Target Doctor Who Library

TARGET

Published in Great Britain in 1988 by
Target Books
An imprint of Virgin Publishing
338 Ladbroke Grove
London W10 5AH

Reprinted 1991

First published in Great Britain in 1987 by
W H Allen and Co PLC

Novelisation copyright © Pip and Jane Baker 1987
Original script copyright © Pip and Jane Baker 1987
'Doctor Who' series copyright © British Broadcasting
Corporation 1987

The BBC producer of *Time and the Rani* was
John Nathan-Turner, the director was Andrew Morgan
The role of the Doctor was played by Sylvester McCoy

Printed and bound in Great Britain by
Cox & Wyman Ltd, Reading

ISBN 0 426 20232 5

1

Regeneration

'Fifty-two . . . fifty-three . . . fifty –'

'Stop skipping, Mel!'

'Doctor, just because you don't object to being over-weight is no reason why I should –'

'Don't argue! Stop!'

Contritely, Mel obeyed: an unusual occurrence. This young companion had a mind of her own, and keeping fit was a dedicated ritual. But there was urgency in the Doctor's tone and a troubled frown on his chubby countenance.

'What is it?'

'I don't know.' He ruffled his mop of fair curls as he studied the console. 'The slide control for setting time and space co-ordinates seems to be stuck!'

Mel, joining him, squinted above the slide control to the read-out displays for stabilising planes. 'This isn't operational either.'

'Take a look at the computer read-out screen.'

'Blank! I'll run a check on the circuit.' On Earth Mel had worked as a computer analyst before becoming the Doctor's companion. But expert or not, she could get no response from the computer read-out.

His patchwork coat-tail flying, the Doctor dashed round the hexagonal console to the Hostile Action Displacement System which he had neglected to set.

Too late!

The TARDIS bucked, throwing him to the floor and sending the unanchored Mel slithering across the control room.

'What's happening, Doctor! What's happening?'

Against a blackcloth of infinite ebony, the TARDIS was being bombarded.

Bolts of multicoloured energy, a fragmented rainbow, strafed the navy-blue police box, tossing it hither and thither. An inharmonious cacophony of sound underscored each salvo.

Mel's slim frame was pitched from the wall to the console. The Doctor, frantically trying to get to his feet, was cast down again by the sickening, unpredictable lurches.

Worse was to come. The whole interior of the TARDIS began undulating and distorting.

Assaulted by the dissonant bedlam, propelled violently from side to side by the giddy oscillations, Mel collapsed near her overturned exercise bike shortly before the Doctor spun reeling, head first, into the plinth of the console.

Both remained unmoving as, almost indiscernible through the jarring discord of sound, the materialisation bellow began.

The TARDIS had been forced into a landing.

But where?

And by whom?

Someone had obviously overridden the TARDIS's sophisticated mechanism and abducted it. For wherever the Doctor had intended visiting, it was certainly not this barren planet.

Barren, indeed, was an appropriate description of Lakertya. Treeless, boulder-strewn, ridged by grassless stratified granite cliffs, it was as colourless and uninviting as the undistinguished concrete blocks of high-rise flats proliferating in some cities on Mel's twentieth-century Earth. The human architects there tried to relieve that soulless vista with propitiously-planted flowering shrubs and garden beds. The Lakertyan landscape nurtured no flowers. At least, not in the rocky terrain on which the TARDIS had fetched up.

There was colour, though, on this grey planet.

The golden profile of a Lakertyan was etched against the skyline. Attracted by the disjointed racket, Ikona, crouched on a cliff edge, was staring at the strange box materialising in the valley below. Mother-of-pearl scales impinged upon his almost perfect features, which were also complemented by a mane of spiky, golden hair. Although his tall figure, cloaked in a saffron yellow tabard, was predominantly humanoid, there was a hint that Lakertyans had a serpentine ancestry at some stage in their evolution. There was a hint, too, of the remnant of a lizard-like tail, hidden beneath the peach cape hanging from his broad shoulders.

Obviously intrigued by the noisy arrival of this phenomenon, Ikona nevertheless maintained a watching brief.

Inside the TARDIS, all was still: the sole sound now was the regular breathing of the two unconscious travellers.

Mel, at full stretch, lay against the wall. The Doctor, lying on his front, was partly concealed by the console. Only his yellow and black striped trousers, flamboyant coat and familiar spats and sneakers were in evidence.

The outside door opened.

Poised on the threshold, clutching what appeared to be a futuristic harpoon gun, was a vision in scarlet.

Tight trews hugged svelte hips before tapering into knee-length boots. A shimmering brocade jacket, its stiff-edged epaulettes trimmed with gold, was belted into a slender waist before flaring into a peplum. Long brunette tresses framed a beautifully sculptured face.

This was the Rani.

The Time Lady who had crossed swords with the Doctor in the past. A renegade whom the Doctor considered to be more brilliant than himself: a compliment he was reluctant to pay since the Rani's brilliance was devoted to the pursuit of scientific knowledge regardless of its repercussions upon man or beast, or any other species she encountered in the Universe.

Arrogantly, the Rani strode to the Doctor's comatose form.

'Leave the girl!' she muttered. From the corner of her eye she had seen a hair-sheathed, scrawny, oily limb extending towards Mel.

The three-taloned paw was snatched away as the recipient of the order glanced at the Rani. But the Rani was only part of the picture the creature saw. It also saw the door behind and the walls at both sides: a quartered, three hundred and sixty degree aspect of the control room was presented simultaneously.

'It's the man I want!' continued the Rani.

The quadview merged into one aspect concentrating on the Doctor.

'Take him to my laboratory,' came the final instruction before she departed.

The prehensile claw reaching forward had a downy membrane connecting each bony digit from below the knuckle joint, leaving the upper portion of two fingers and a thumb free.

It tugged roughly at the Time Lord's shoulder, rolling him onto his back so that he was face up.

Face up?

But these were not the rotund features of the Doctor. This face was small and delicately pointed. And the clothes! They were the Doctor's certainly, and his

8

multi-coloured furled umbrella hung over his shoulders. Yet the erstwhile tightly-buttoned plaid waistcoat hung in folds, the spotted cravat sagged about a thin neck with its bow drooping over a narrow chest, and the sleeves of the exotic coat now flopped beyond the ends of his short arms.

Could this be the endearing sixth Time Lord?

The Rani had no doubt. A single look was all the confirmation she needed. And she would not be mistaken.

In fact, there was no mistake.

This was, indeed, the Doctor. Regeneration had been triggered by the tumultuous buffeting.

In consequence, the seventh Doctor was now in the clutches of the Rani and her obscene collaborator . . .

2

The New Doctor

'Leave the girl!' the Rani had said, intending to deal with Mel later.

A shadow fell across the still unmoving Mel. Was she now to be cradled in those crooked, downy arms?

But the hand that reached towards her could have been human except for the fact that the skin was golden with mother-of-pearl scales which encroached upon the wrist that poked from a saffron yellow sleeve.

Ikona squatted beside the extraterrestial visitor. Grimacing with repugnance, he pinched her flushed cheek and tugged her curly red hair. A low hiss of displeasure accompanied each touch.

Then, abruptly rubbing his palms on his tabard as though to wipe away the revulsion he felt from the contact, Ikona snatched up the unconscious Mel, brusquely hoisted her over his shoulder, and padded from the control room.

Eyes closed, the prostrate Doctor reclined on a workbench.

Grouped symmetrically about the bench, as if at the points of the compass, were four small pyramids, each the height of the Doctor's TARDIS.

The pyramid in the north corner was a crystal tank containing a fermenting 'soup' of a speckled magenta and grey glutinous liquid. The east and west pyramids housed megabyte computers whose gauges and digital logs were inert.

However, the most intriguing pyramid of the quartet sat at the south corner: it bore a gaping, charred hole that was evidence of an internal explosion.

Had they been functioning, the triangular machines would have been processing and then feeding the magenta, glutinous goo through the rear wall, the curvature of which indicated it was a section of a spherical chamber.

The Doctor was aware of none of this. Consciousness had not yet returned.

Nor was the Rani in the lab with him.

She was in an adjacent, sombre arcade which was crudely hewn into the subterranean rock of a gully that housed the complete laboratory suite.

The narrow, claustrophobic arcade was lined with offset cabinets let into the thick walls. Through the glass fronts of the reclining sarcophagi it was possible to discern that ten of them were occupied. Two were not. And the Rani was concentrating on one of these.

'Get him inside. Quickly!'

She was addressing two Lakertyans. Sarn, a young female, nervously exhibited trepidation. Beyus, a tall, regal, older male, showed only disapproval at the task allotted them. For the 'him' they were incarcerating in the cabinet was a man from Earth: a genius from the twentieth century whose shock of hair and bushy moustache would render him immediately recognisable to any student of science. This was Professor Albert Einstein: the originator of the theory of relativity and father of nuclear physics.

The Rani had returned to Earth in her TARDIS, plucked him out of Time and transported him to Lakertya, to the arcade, where his anaesthetised form was now being installed in the eleventh cabinet.

'The collar, Beyus!'

Beyus clamped a polyethylene collar about Einstein's

12

neck. His forehead puckering with distaste, he plugged first a cable and then a transparent tube into the collar.

Sarn's clumsy efforts at assisting him hindered rather than helped.

'Stop dithering!' the Rani snapped.

'I – I don't want to harm him –'

Impatiently, the Rani thrust the timid Sarn aside. 'Seal it and label it,' she told Beyus.

He closed the glass front then stood, artlessly looking at the Rani.

'What're you waiting for?' she asked.

'You've not given me the name for the label.'

'Einstein.' The voice was cutting. 'Such insolence could cost your people dearly, Beyus.'

The threat alarmed the timorous Sarn. 'I am sure Beyus did not mean to appear insolent. He . . . would . . . never do . . . that . . .' Her brave defence faltered under the Rani's cold appraisal.

'I find your incompetence more than enough without listening to your puerile opinions.'

'Then why not let Sarn go? You've got me as hostage. You don't need her.' He laid a comforting arm about the young female's cowering shoulders.

'*I* shall decide my needs. They, unfortunately, require the use of Lakertyans.'

'You've left me with no illusions about the hatred you hold for us.'

'Hatred? Another fantasy. I've no feelings one way or the other. Outside my experiments, you have absolutely no significance.'

'Your detachment is difficult to understand.'

'All you need understand is that these specimens are geniuses!' She began strolling the length of the cabinets. Each was labelled. The names *Louis Pasteur* and *Charles Darwin* were alongside those of less familiar luminaries

13

culled from galaxies throughout the Universe: *Za Panato*, *Ari Centos* and others.

'And if they're not kept in prime condition,' she continued as she checked the dials on the glass fronts, 'you'll have more than the skin of *this* bungling novice to worry about!'

Shaking with fear, Sarn hid behind Beyus who was attending to the tubes and cables looping from the tops of the cabinets. Merged together, they were channelled, via a conduit, into the laboratory and then distributed among the pyramidal machines.

The Rani moved towards the door.

'Have you managed to procure the means to repair your laboratory apparatus?'

'Procure?' The Rani smiled. 'Procured, yes indeed!'

Beyus straightened the plaited black and gold band circling his skull. The joke was incomprehensible but its import was not: the Rani had obviously achieved her objective.

As she entered the lab, that objective was still sleeping on a bench.

The Rani listened to his first heart and then to his second; for Time Lords have two hearts.

In an impassive assessment of his condition she lifted his eyelids to inspect his pupils.

Assured of his continuing unconscious state, she turned her attention to the spherical chamber and punched out a number on a combination lock.

A panel glided open . . .

Palpitating magenta light bathed her haughty features and, attuned to the pulsations was a sinister, pervading throbbing.

The Rani seemed exalted, but the light's influence on the lab was baleful. Even the Doctor's pleasant features appeared misshapen and gargoylish as they were

14

swamped by the sickly purple.

Almost as if he sensed the evil atmosphere, he groaned and stirred. Immediately alerted, the Rani shut the panel, cutting off the purple light, and crossed over to him.

On the knife-edge of consciousness, he blinked. 'Ah, that was a nice nap.' He struggled from the bench. 'Down to business. I'm a bit worried about the temporal flicker in Sector Thirteen; there's a bicentennial refit to book in for the TARDIS; must just pop over to Centauri Seven and then perhaps a quick holiday. Right. That all seems quite clear. Just three small points – where am I? . . . Who am I?' Trying to unscramble his muddled wits, he registered the Rani's presence: 'And who are you? . . . You! The Rani!'

He shied away from her, but in his weakened condition his movements were unco-ordinated.

Tottering, he grabbed a stool.

'Stay back! Stay back!'

Flourishing the stool with all the majesty of his supposed six-feet height, he overreached himself and toppled – all five-feet-six of him – against the machine.

'This is idiotic. You'll injure yourself,' she said.

'Why should you care? Complete indifference to the welfare of others is your hallmark.' A true summation of the Rani's usual attitude. 'Since you were exiled from Gallifrey, you've had nothing but contempt for all Time Lords.' Gallifrey was the home of the Time Lords.

'My contempt started before my exile.'

'Then why the solicitude? What is it you want from me? And where's Mel?' He peered warily about, trying to acclimatise. In an attempt to rise, he reeled into a monitor. 'I can't think . . . everything's jumbled.'

'You're still concussed –'

'Where's Mel?'

The ferocity of the demand punctured the Rani's

charade of compassion. 'She's perfectly safe. But how long that remains so depends on you!'

After a wild, pointless parry with the stool, he jabbed at the buttons displayed beneath the monitor screen. 'You'll be up to something. Perhaps I'll get the answer from this.'

The screen brightened, showing a planet being orbited by a dark, forbidding asteroid. A series of calculations were tabulated at the base of the screen.

'You won't recognise the planet. It's Lakertya. And there's no evidence it's ever been graced by your meddling presence!'

'And you're trying to divert me. So the answer *is* on here.' He pondered the calculations. 'Quarks . . . one up . . . one down . . . one Strange Matter!' Genuinely shocked, he glared bleakly at the Rani. 'That asteroid's composed of Strange Matter! What monstrous experiment are you dabbling in now?'

'I didn't go to the trouble of bringing you here to discuss the ethics of my work.' Her calm was juxtaposed with the Doctor's agitation.

'Ethics! Don't be a hypocrite! Your past is littered with the mutilated results of unethical experiments.'

'Save the cant! I had all I could take of that in our university days.' The Rani and the Doctor had attended the same university as students: she specialised in neurochemistry, he in thermodynamics. It was his tutored expertise she needed, but she chose not to reveal the truth yet. 'Am I expected to abandon my research because of the side-effects on inferior species?' Selecting a syringe from a rack, she squirted a drop from its needle, ensuring it was ready for use. 'Are you prepared to abandon walking in the fields lest you squash an insect underfoot?' She advanced on the Doctor, syringe to the fore.

Her icy logic found no echo in the Doctor. 'Stay away

from me! Whatever you've brought me here for, I'm having no part of! None at all!'

Having disposed of the stool while operating the computer screen, his only defence was his umbrella which had been brought from the TARDIS. Brandishing it like a rapier, he floundered towards the arcade door, pushing it wide in his bid for escape – to be confronted by Beyus and Sarn.

The suddenness of the encounter, the surprise at the unusual appearance of the golden-maned Lakertyans, caused him to recoil. Unfortunately, his trousers being far too long, his heel got entangled in the overlapping hem and tripped him!

Despite the fact that he was to Sarn a weird alien, the gentle Lakertyan automatically went to his aid.

'Leave him there!' the Rani ordered.

'He may be hurt.'

Beyus, older and wiser, realised the Rani would brook no disobedience. 'Sarn, don't interfere!'

However, ignoring them both, Sarn assisted the Doctor to his feet. Off balance, he staggered towards the crystal tank.

Savagely, the Rani, syringe at the ready, elbowed Sarn aside, sending her spinning across the lab. 'That's the last time you'll ever interfere!' The finality in her voice left neither Sarn nor Beyus in any doubt that the young Lakertyan's life was in jeopardy.

'Stay away from me or I'll smash this!' The Doctor rapped the crystal tank with the ferrule of his umbrella. 'I'll smash it to pieces!' The umbrella was clutched, ready to be wielded like an axe.

'Are you willing to sacrifice your companion as well?' asked the Rani coolly, implying that she held Mel in custody.

The Doctor hesitated, but even so he was firm in his reply. 'Yes. Both of us if need be. Fraternising with you could put more than just the two of us at risk!' He was referring to the awesome power inherent in the Strange Matter asteroid.

'Oh, spare me the high-minded moralising!'

'Spare the rod and spoil the broth.' The Doctor stopped, confused. 'I mean, spoil the –'

'And I can do without your feeble attempts at humour.'

Feeble it may have been, but it was no attempt at humour. The Doctor was genuinely mixed up.

The exchange, though, did provide sufficient diversion for Sarn to slip surreptitiously through the exit leading to the outside.

'Urak!' The Rani's concentration was entirely on the Doctor. 'Urak! Get in here!'

Held in an oily, hair-matted claw, a silver-tubed gun jutted from the arcade.

A click.

From the sleek barrel in a shower of sparks came a wispy, electronic net. With devastating accuracy, it hovered above the Doctor . . . then floated down . . .

Shrouded in the glittering web, the Doctor fell to the lab floor.

Stunned.

Once again at the Rani's mercy.

3

Death Is Sprung

With fleeting glances to check whether she was being pursued, Sarn fled along a rutted path bisecting the hinterland beyond the Rani's laboratory complex.

In her panic, she failed to seek the easiest route, stumbling over loose shale despite her lizard-like sure-footedness. But grazed and bruised ankles could not stop Sarn. She knew from grim experience that the only hope of avoiding death was to hide from the Rani.

A warning light flashed in the lab, and a siren began to wail.

'The female Sarn . . . has escaped . . . Mistress Rani . . .' Urak's voice was low-pitched and resonant, with exaggerated emphasis on the hard 't', 'd', and 's' consonants. The cadence, too, had an odd peculiarity: a pause after every three or four beats.

The Rani cast an irritated look at the stunned Doctor who was again lying on the bench: his tomfoolery had precipitated this situation!

'She won't get far!'

Nor had she. Lack of stamina was slowing Sarn and her distress had escalated. Not only did the windswept path afford scant protection, but the caterwauling of the siren primed her fear: the hunt was on in earnest.

The wail of the siren perturbed Ikona too. Unaware of its cause, or that he was heading towards the absconding Sarn, he wended through monoliths of jagged granite, the insensible Mel humped over his shoulder.

Gazing about for cover, he failed to detect that Mel was beginning to regain her faculties. Her sudden resistance threw him off-balance. Kicking and pummelling, she managed to break free.

Benefiting from her superb fitness, Mel quickly outstripped Ikona. Haring round a bend, she came to an abrupt halt.

So did Sarn.

Mel's physical appearance was similar to the Rani's!

Hissing with horror, Sarn scampered from the path.

Her shin hit a trip-wire, triggering a tremendous *whoosh!* Dust and gravel exploded skywards, temporarily blurring the golden figure.

When the dust settled, a huge, plastic, opaque bubble had formed about Sarn, imprisoning her. Attached to it, like a tumour, was a bulging metal plate. A jet of stream issued from its underside.

For a brief moment Sarn could be seen crouched inside – then the bubble began to spin . . . and spin . . . until, velocity surging, it shot forward, rolling faster and faster, out of control. Spinning from the path – it crashed into a craggy rock.

At the instant of impact, an incandescent, glowing heat spread from the metal plate, engulfing the bubble and its captive.

Illuminated by the white heat, Mel was forced to shield her face and avert her gaze. When, as the heat abated, she dared to look, Ikona was alongside her.

But he paid Mel no heed.

His steps faltering, brows drawn in anguish, he continued past her to where the explosion had taken place.

All that remained of his young compatriot was an ivory skeleton.

On a monitor screen in the lab, a diminishing blob glowed in a section of the superimposed grid informing

20

the Rani that a security device had been detonated.

'See the trap is reset,' she said to Urak.

'Certainly . . .' came the obsequious reply. 'Your powers are . . . truly wondrous . . . Mistress Rani . . .'

Flicking off the monitor screen, she collected the high-pressure syringe and applied it to the still-stunned Doctor's wrist.

'What are you . . . doing, Mistress?'

From Urak's elliptical quadview, the Rani's actions, the door to the arcade, the panel of the spherical chamber and the exit to the grounds were all visible at once. As she spoke, the latter three aspects were blanked out and only the Rani's image remained.

'Making certain he suffers a healthy dose of amnesia when he wakes.'

'What is it . . . you do not . . . want him to . . . remember?'

'That doesn't concern you. Go and fetch the girl.'

'I did not mean . . . to offend, Mis . . . tress. If I . . . seek knowledge, it . . . is only to . . . benefit from . . . your great and . . . wonderful wisdom –'

'Oh, get on with it!' Flattery was wasted on the Rani. 'Fetch the girl!'

The girl she referred to, of course, was the Doctor's companion, Mel.

Benumbed by the trauma of the event she had just witnessed, she stared down at Sarn's pathetic remains.

Ikona, incensed by grief, berated her. 'Go on – run!'

She backed off, unsure what to do: her erstwhile kidnapper now seemed to be urging her to escape.

Or was he? By circling, he was restricting her choice, ensuring her sole line of retreat was in the same direction as Sarn had taken.

'Run? The grounds are full of traps!' she cried. Ikona feinted a lunge, causing her to retreat onto the path. 'As well you know!'

'Me? Why should I? This is insane!' cried Mel.

'Don't play the innocent, you bloodthirsty alien! Your friends set those traps!' Another lunge, this time for the throat!

Pulling away, she slipped and rolled from the path into a ditch. Fearful lest another trap should be sprung, she stood up, keeping an arm's length away from the angry Ikona. 'Please, I can understand your being upset!'

'Upset! Yet another of your obscene murders takes place and you –'

'Will you stop accusing me!' Mel's temper rose, matching his. 'This had nothing to do with me!'

'Lies! If I didn't need you as a hostage, you'd be dead!'

Mel was flummoxed. She'd been knocked out by the turbulence in the TARDIS, come to on the shoulders of this odd creature, and now was being told she was to be used as a hostage! 'A hostage? For what?'

'To exchange for our leader. Your friends took him prisoner.'

Friends? What friends, thought the bewildered Mel. The only friend she had was the Doctor and he, presumably, was in the TARDIS. 'Why do you keep calling them friends of mine?'

'You arrived from out of space as they did.' A sudden, unexpected grab deceived her.' Well they can have you back! On *my* terms!'

She tried to scream, but the arm embracing her neck was jammed against her larynx.

Wriggling only demonstrated that his strength was far superior to hers: every squirm simply increased the pressure on her windpipe.

Acquiescence became a requirement of survival as the implacable Ikona untied a rope from his waist.

22

4

Identity Crisis

The laboratory had two occupants: the Doctor prostrate on the bench, and the red-haired girl standing with her back to him.

She was bent almost double examining the ripped hole in the machine, but the white trews, pink and white striped long-sleeved tight-waisted bolero and matching striped ankle warmers, made her easily identifiable as Mel.

The Doctor stirred. Blinked. Perplexed, he scanned, without recognition, the lab. He frowned, willing himself to remember. But his memory seemed to have been wiped clean. 'Where am I? Who are you?'

'Mel. Melanie.' The girl turned.

The costume was identical to Mel's – the white sneakers, the candy-striped blouse, even the puffed leg-of-mutton sleeves. But the mass of red hair did not embellish the pert, elfin-like face of Mel. These red curls framed the classical features of the Rani!

'Are you all right, Doctor?' The Rani even mimicked Mel's voice and perky manner.

'All right? Am I? Of course. Of course.' He sat up. 'Are you?'

'Me? Yes. Why not?'

'Indeed, why not? We both are.' Exhibiting bravado, he boldly got off the bench.

Too boldly! His knees buckled, causing him to stagger. The Rani tried to help him but his weight was too much and they floundered together drunkenly, every which way. The 'Mel' smile she had adopted wilted as she was torn between supporting him and saving her precious equipment when he collided into it.

'Oops!' he exclaimed. 'A bull in a barber's shop.'

A barber's shop? This was the second proverb he had misquoted: certainly a reversal of his sixth persona when he had a quotation for all occasions, but ones which were usually word perfect.

The Rani's innate priorities asserted themselves. She abandoned the Doctor and concentrated on preserving the flasks, pipettes, and other delicate apparatus which were in danger of being smashed.

Eventually, legs sagging, the Doctor clutched a pyramid for support. Steadied at last, his attention strayed to the futuristic custom-built harpoon gun. 'A Navigational Guidance System Distorter! That'd suck any passing space-craft out of the sky.' True. He did not know it, but this was the very means which had been used to bring the TARDIS into the Rani's orbit. 'Er – where are we?'

'In your lab on Lakertya. Doctor, are you sure you're well?'

'Certainly. Certainly. Fit as a trombone.'

'Fiddle!'

'Mmm?'

'Fit as a fiddle!' the Rani snapped.

'Fiddle? Yes. Nerves, I expect.' His fingers were twitching under the over-long sleeves. He concertinaed the cuffs, absently rubbing his wrist where the injection needle had punctured the skin. 'Now, let's see . . . what were we up to – er – Mel, did you say your name was?'

'You don't remember me, do you?' She did not waver from her adopted role, but her eyes searched keenly for any sign of memory revival. 'You don't, do you?' If the fool didn't accept her as Mel, then she'd gone to a lot of trouble for nothing! It gave her no pleasure to wear this ridiculous wig and cute clothes!

'Red hair . . . I recall red hair –' he stopped, horrified. 'What's that!' His wanderings had taken him to a full-length mirror in which both he and 'Mel' were reflected.

'Not what. Who. It's me.'

'*With* you, I mean.'

'That's you, Doctor.'

'*Me!*' Shocked, unbelieving, he patted his head, seeking the familiar mop of fair curls . . . but he tousled only short, sleek, dark hair. The mirror image copied, confirming the worst! 'No wonder I've lost my memory!'

The Rani's tolerance was wearing thin. 'Never mind the pathos!' Realising the Mel characterisation was slipping, she faked a sweet smile. 'I mean, you're supposed to be conducting an experiment. Not frightening yourself to death.'

'Experiment?'

She indicated the ravaged machine in the south pyramid. 'It exploded and threw you to the ground; me too. Knocked both of us cold. When I came round' – she shrugged *à la* Mel – 'you were as you look now.'

'The shock of the explosion must have caused me to regenerate.'

'You mean, this is what you're going to look like permanently?' She was unable to resist turning the screw!

'I want all mirrors removed from the TARDIS henceforth!' he cried, definitely not enamoured of his changed appearance!

'Oh, so you recall the TARDIS then?' Apprehension modified her tone: was the drug's potency on the wane? Unobtrusively, she picked up a syringe ready to inject a booster if necessary.

'The TARDIS? . . . Yes. And you, Mel. Yet . . .' –
gawping at her – '. . . there's something out of sync
. . .' He shook himself. 'I'm obviously experiencing
post-regeneration amnesia.'

'Don't worry. It'll pass.' She replaced the syringe.
'Meanwhile, why not repair the machine? You said it
was important.'

'Important? Did I? Wonder what I was up to?' He
squinted into the hole. 'Seems pretty far gone. Need a
genius to unravel this.'

'Well, you are a genius.'

'Yes . . . Yes. I can definitely remember that.'

'Especially in thermodynamics.'

'How did you know that, Mel?'

'You told me. It was your special subject when you
were at university.'

'University . . .' The reference seemed to strike a
vague chord of memory. 'You remind me of someone I
knew when I was there . . .'

The Rani cut in hurriedly. 'The machine, Doctor. It
has to be repaired. And you're the only one with the
particular skills to do it.'

'Your confidence is very flattering, Mel.' He poked
his head into the charred hole.

The real Mel's head was poked into something too: a
halter!

In a rough tug-of-war, she was being un-
ceremoniously hauled along by Ikona through a narrow
canyon. The rope hobbling her ankles and tethering her
wrists was also a noose about her neck! Ikona intended
keeping a firm hold on his to-be-traded-in hostage.

'I'm choking,' gasped Mel.

No response from the determined captor.

'D'you hear? I'm choking!'

'Then stop struggling.'

26

Reinforcing his lack of sympathy, he jerked the halter to maintain pace.

An obdurate scowl from Mel. 'Will you listen! How many more times do I have to repeat I'm not your enemy!'

'I'd prefer you to say nothing. Your endless squawking hurts my ears.'

'I'm not mad about you either,' countered Mel. 'But trading insults isn't going to get us anywhere.'

Another fierce jerk caused her to stumble and almost fall.

'Look – can we begin from scratch? My name's Mel and I come from Earth. Your turn.'

'This is no game, Earthling.'

'Okay.' A sigh. 'Let's try another tack. You claim I was alone when you found me.'

'Don't start on about this mythical Doctor again!' This was at least the fifth occasion on which Mel had asked about the Doctor.

'I have to!'

'There was no one else in the strange box. If he exists' – and, in Ikona's cynical opinion, she was lying – 'he must have left.'

'Not a chance! The Doctor wouldn't've left me!'

'If he had any sense he would!'

'It's not even up for discussion!'

'Good. I shall enjoy the silence!'

The silence did not last long.

Dragged mercilessly over loose stones and boulders, the hobbled Mel's attention, unlike Ikona's, was on the perilous terrain. A lucky break for Ikona.

'Watch out!' she yelled.

Determination in every stride, Ikona had not spotted a mine buried in the shale.

The warning came fractionally too late. His leather-clad foot made contact with the mine.

27

Simultaneously, Mel gave a tremendous yank on the rope.

Huddled together, petrified spectators, they watched the formation of the opaque bubble. Would the volatile fireball spin towards them?

By the grace of good fortune, the contraption was propelled away from them into the cliffside. The explosion sent fragmented rock and dust spiralling. The canyon reverberated, amplifying the ear-splitting detonation.

Spluttering in the dust cloud, Mel extricated herself from Ikona.

'Now will you accept I'm not your enemy?'

Ikona's response was to begin untying her bond. 'We must hurry. The Tetraps will come to investigate.'

Tetraps? Mel had never heard the name. But she put the question on hold: it was imperative for her to win the confidence of Ikona.

'What made you think I was in league with them?'

'You're not Lakertyan. You don't belong on this planet.'

'They're human?' queried Mel, surprised. 'Like me?'

His reply surprised her even more.

'Not like you. Although they are almost as hideous.' There was no doubting the sincerity of his statement!

Despite the fraught situation she was in, Mel felt affronted. Ignorant of his *faux pas*, Ikona scaled an awkward crevase and then turned, with an oddly lizard-like, stiff-necked movement, to ensure that Mel was following.

She began the tricky ascent. 'Just as well I'm wearing sneakers,' she muttered to herself. She preferred the more fashionable high-heeled boots she had worn with her previous pants suit. As it happened, she had been exercising when the disaster overcame the TARDIS,

28

and so she was appropriately dressed for this inhospitable planet beneath its cerise sky: inhospitable,
that is, unless you enjoy Lakertyan reptilian ancestry!

Thoughts of the TARDIS made her wonder about
the Doctor. Where was he? What had befallen him?
Was he a prisoner? If so, of whom?

Had she looked back, her speculation would have
been less on the Doctor's safety and more on her own.

Several hundred metres to the rear, a hairy, bony
claw eased over a rock.

Urak, having gone to the TARDIS and found Mel no
longer there, had picked up the spores of the missing
girl . . . and was in dedicated pursuit . . .

5

Collaborators All

Fitness fanatic though she might be, Mel's resources were being taxed by Ikona's zealous flight.

'Hey, put on the brakes! I need a breather!'

'We must keep moving.' Ikona knew the thunderclap from the trap he had set off would have alerted the enemy.

A perceptive deduction: Urak was already trailing them.

The Tetrap's quadview encompassed cliffs to his rear, a crevasse to his right, a canyon to his left, and a boulder-strewn plateau in front of him. In none of them did Ikona and Mel feature.

Every granite outcrop, every niche in the rocks, seemed to harbour menace as Mel darted between them. Ikona reduced his pace in deference to her pleas, but his anxiety was evident.

'What happened to the rest of your people?' Mel queried. 'Wouldn't they help?'

'No. They've been completely subdued.'

Mel, registering the bitterness, nevertheless persisted. 'We could at least ask them.'

'The only one they listen to is Beyus, our leader.'

'Fine, let's go to him.'

'He's the hostage I wanted to exchange you for – Listen!'

They froze.

Listened. Sure enough, far off but getting ominously nearer, were the faint sounds of pursuit.

Breaking from cover, Ikona struck out for the wide expanse of the plateau.

'We can't go that way! It's completely exposed!' Mel wanted to stay hidden.

'For once don't argue!' he ordered. 'Quickly!'

Feeling increasingly vulnerable, Mel tagged reluctantly along. Her own choice would have been to make for the cliffs and find a cave: she prayed that Ikona knew what he was doing!

He did.

Buried in a gully, its entrance camouflaged by deceptively-arranged sedimentary rock, was a drainage pipe. Shoving Mel ahead of him, Ikona crawled inside his prepared hideaway. 'They'll think we've doubled back to stay under cover,' he predicted.

Mel was less sanguine. 'Always providing they don't flush us out first!'

'Come on! Come on!' The Doctor lifted his perspiring face.

A discharge of sparks had showered from the hole in the machine. The Doctor was using a makeshift acetylene torch to solder broken circuitry.

'Come where?' In ill humour, the Rani surveyed the chaos in the lab. Flex and cable criss-crossed the floor and the crudely-joined tubing for the torch added to the muddle.

'Why I chose you as an assistant, I'll never fathom! Perhaps I will when I've regained my memory.'

'What is it you want?'

'Look at me! Can't you see? Mop my brow!'

With bad grace, the Rani produced a silk handkerchief and dabbed his brow. Moving away, her dignity suffered another blow. Irately, the Doctor tugged at the tubing, unwittingly causing it to loop round her sneakers, almost upending her.

'Watch where you're going!'

Fighting to curb her temper, she dumped the offensive handkerchief in a wastebin beneath the rack of vials. 'It was your fault!' she snapped.

'Bad workmen always blame their fools.'

'Tools! Blame their tools!' The idiot was really proving a trial! If only she didn't need his expertise . . .

'Do I detect a hint of displeasure, Mel? This egalitarian spirit doesn't strike a note of harmony.' Another shower of sparks erupted from the hole. 'Or could it be you think yourself superior to me?'

The Rani's tapered fingers caressed a vial bearing the legend *cyanide* . . . 'How could I possibly assume that, Doctor?' It took every ounce of self-control to maintain the meek role she had opted to play.

'Quite. Although I feel far from superior at the moment. This is all a mystery to me.'

The soldering stopped.

'Surely there's a catalyst in there,' she encouraged.

'Yes. Yes,' he chided, quitting the machine. 'Must you state the obvious? I'm well aware that its function is to fuse the impulses from there' – indicating the conduit – 'with this goo.' He dipped his thumb into the crystal tank. 'But what's it all for!' He studied the thumb as though the answer might be written there. 'I'm beginning to think this set-up had nothing to do with me.'

'Why's that?' she asked, apprehension usurping vexation.

'Omnipotence. The mind responsible for this bag of tricks operates on a grand scale.'

Inwardly she cursed his prescience. At all costs he must be prevented from discovering the secret of the spherical chamber.

'All the more reason why it should be you, Doctor.'

'Then . . . why do I have such an overwhelming sense of foreboding . . .' His perturbed gaze strayed from contemplation of the mass of tubes and apparatus to the door of the arcade.

Weighed down by a yoke from which dangled two buckets of red liquid, Beyus passed the cabinet entombing Louis Pasteur.

A thumping on the arcade door startled him.

'Why is this door locked?' The Doctor's demand could be clearly heard.

So could the Rani's reply. 'You locked it.'

'I did?' came the incredulous response.

Careful not to slop the plasma, Beyus continued on his unsavoury errand.

Having been baulked by the arcade door, the Doctor, in high dudgeon, strutted to the panel of the spherical chamber. 'Is this locked too?'

Repairing the machine had been entirely forgotten, much to the Rani's chagrin.

'You – and only you – know the combination number.' Humouring the fractious dupe, she decided, was the best means of coaxing him to work.

'What's in there?'

'I've no idea.'

With random jabs, he tried to operate the combination lock. Irritated at his lack of success, he embarked on a tour of investigation which ended when his foot became snared in the mess of cables. Frustration boiled over into petulance.

'You seem very adept in the art of ignorance, Mel. Are you as clueless as you appear?'

'Don't blame me, Doctor. I've never been inside. You wouldn't let me.'

'Wouldn't I?'

'You said the air wasn't sterile enough for humans.'

Disentangling his foot from the cable, he squatted on

the edge of the bench. 'That's it then!' He folded his arms. 'I'm doing nothing more until my memory returns. Nothing until I know what I'm about. I won't work in the dark like this. No! No! I'm finished!'

Patience and tolerance were not virtues the Rani cultivated, but she had to exercise both in this circumstance. 'Oh, come on, now,' she wheedled. 'You thrive on challenge. And you're the only one with the knowledge to repair the machine.'

This last statement was genuine: it was part of the reason for hijacking the TARDIS and bringing the meddlesome Time Lord to Lakertya.

He refused to be appeased. 'No, I'm adamant! This could be some diabolical scheme.'

A prophetic conclusion.

He was yet to learn how prophetic.

An unwilling collaborator in the 'diabolical scheme' was at that moment performing a ritual that never ceased to be an ordeal.

The yoke cutting into his shoulders beneath the lime green tabard trimmed with an orange cloak draped across his tall form, Beyus entered the portal of a tenebrous underground eyrie. The menial task he had been allotted, ill-fitted his status as the Chief Functionary of the Lakertyans. Yet he was performing it without protest.

Bracing himself, he lifted a barred grating and descended into the eyrie.

Vaguely discernible in the gloom were indistinct brown shapes, some two metres long, hanging from the rafters. In the steamy, fetid fug, an occasional rustle added to the macabre atmosphere.

Averting his eyes, Beyus emptied the buckets into a hopper. The thick, red, revolting mixture oozed its noisome way down a chute to a feeding trough.

As its nauseous smell wafted to the rafters, a more
excited rustling disturbed the rancid darkness . . .

6

On With The Fray

It was dark and musty, too, inside the drainpipe.

And cramped. Especially for Ikona's lanky frame. Doubled over, he hugged his leather-thonged legs to his chest.

Mel's petite form was more compatible with the confined space, but the claustrophobic atmosphere and the waiting were galling. 'Do you think –'

Ikona's golden palm clapped over her mouth. The hollowness of the pipe magnified every sound and Ikona knew Urak would not yet have given up the chase.

Nor had he.

His three hundred and sixty degree view of the plateau betrayed no living beings.

Not easily deterred, Urak, ears cocked, stood motionless, his muscular, prehensile feet centimetres from the concealed access to the drain . . .

'Here, drink this!' The Rani's patience strained at the leash.

The Doctor, obdurately ensconced on the bench, had not relented from his refusal to continue repairing the machine.

'You're just over-excited. It'll calm you down.'

He accepted the tumbler she was profferring. 'What is it?'

'Only water.'

'Hmmmm.' Absently he tipped the contents into the

sink.

A fortuitous act. Water it certainly was, but the Rani had spiked it with an hypnoidal inducer while he was gazing dolefully at the spherical chamber.

'Don't try to placate me! Leave me alone!'

'You can't just loll around, Doctor. It's simply not like you!'

'How do you know what I'm like? I've regenerated.' He waggled his overlong sleeves, hoisted up the trousers sagging from his waistline. 'Look at me! Look at me!'

'You've changed outwardly, but you must have the same sweet nature.' The Rani almost gagged as she uttered the last three words, but desperation beckoned.

'Perhaps this is my new persona. Sulky. Bad-tempered. Think how I spoke to you earlier.'

'You didn't mean it. *I* was at fault.' Desperation indeed!

'Well, that's probably how I am now. You can't regulate regeneration, Mel. It's a lottery and I've drawn the short straw.'

The Rani did, of course, understand regeneration. Like all Gallifreyans, she had thirteen lives. Unlike the Doctor, she still enjoyed her first. This virtuoso scientist did not believe in taking personal risks. When carrying out her experiments – and many of them were very bizarre – she always devised an antidote or an escape plan to ensure her own survival. In fact, the nearest she had come to forfeiting one of her lives was on her last encounter with the Doctor.

Sent hurtling at ultra-warp speed to the remote regions of the Milky Way, she and that other exiled Time Lord, the Master, had been caged in her TARDIS at the mercy of a carnivorous Tyrannosaurus Rex.

The jar, in which she was preserving it in embryo,

had been smashed and Time Spillage had caused the primeval monster to grow larger by the second. Hungry, lacerating jaws had gaped at the two tasty morsels flattened by centrifugal force against the walls . . . it seemed nothing would prevent the pair of renegades from becoming a dinosaur's snack!

However, the Time Spillage that accelerated the Tyrannosaurus from babyhood into virile youth also accelerated it into full size. Its spine snapped against the ceiling of the TARDIS.

The Master, his megalomania in full spate, had claimed divine indestructibility. But the Rani knew better . . .

'Anyway, I need a radiation wave meter. And versatile as I am, even I can't improvise that!'

The bald statement interrupted the Rani's reverie. This was a new and more hopeful tack. 'What about the TARDIS? Will there be a radiation wave meter there?'

'The TARDIS?' The Doctor rallied. 'D'you know where it is?'

'Yes, of course.'

'I could do with a breath of fresh air. We'll go there together.' Springing from the bench, he pranced from the laboratory.

'Wait –!' Her entreaty went unheeded. The jaunty seventh Doctor had departed.

Before following, she activated the monitor. The screen was divided into four elliptical sections of the plateau.

'Urak!' She edged a mini-computer-bracelet from beneath her sleeve. The device allowed the Rani to communicate with Urak. 'Remove the girl from the TARDIS.' She did not want the Doctor to go blundering into the genuine Mel.

'She is not . . . there, Mistress . . .' A revelation Urak would have preferred to avoid.

'Find her, you incompetent fool!'
'Certainly, Mis . . . tress . . .'

Crouched together, maintaining a dismayed silence, Mel and Ikona could hear Urak's reply: he was that close to their hideaway.

Mel's brown eyes sought reassurance from Ikona. He had none to give. His stern profile with its aquiline nose and protruding, unfurrowed brow, was silhouetted against the curved interior of the drainage pipe: not a muscle stirred beneath the shiny scales fringing his cheeks.

'Come on, Mel!' hollered the Doctor. He was ambling along the path, expansively filling his lungs. The Rani caught him up and passed him, only too happy to get to the TARDIS quickly.

Her haste found no response. Instead the Doctor was engrossed in his surroundings; fascinating virgin territory for him. Blithely disregarding her impatience, he paused to examine the texture of a basalt slab. A few more paces and he spotted the skeleton of Sarn.

It held no sad significance for the Doctor. Not a glimmer of memory recalled the shy and blameless young Lakertyan who had compassionately come to his aid.

'Unusual specimen,' he mused. 'Can't say I recognise it.' The length of the spine intrigued him. 'Humanoid with reptilian influence wouldn't you think, Mel?'

'Lakertyan. A race so indolent they can't even be bothered to bury their dead.' Said in an imitation of Mel's diction, the sentiment was definitely the Rani's!

'Really? I suppose we've explored this planet. I wish I could remember.'

'There's not a lot *to* remember. A benevolent climate and indulgent regime has induced atrophy. They've failed to realise their full potential.'

'Rather a harsh judgment, Mel.'

'Not mine. Yours!' The spite was barely concealed.

'The more I know about me, the less I like . . .' he said bleakly.

'Doctor! Let's get on!'

Mel wanted to get on too. They had heard Urak move away and she was anxious to resume her quest.

'Can we go?'

Head hunched over his knees, Ikona gave no response.

Sighing with irritation, Mel wriggled to the end of the pipe.

Gingerly, mole-like, Mel's mop of curls poked out of the hideaway. A brief, perky peek all around, then, like a gopher popping back into its burrow, she disappeared again. 'No one about. Come on!'

'It is too soon.'

'Not for me. I'm going to find the Doctor.'

'If he's been captured, he's as good as dead.'

The idea sent a shudder through her. 'Were you born a pessimist, or is it self-induced?'

'I'm a realist.'

'At least tell me where he'll be!'

Ikona did not bother to reply.

'All right. I'll find him without you.' She squirmed, on her stomach, from the drain. 'One thing about the Doctor,' she thought as she brushed clinging grit from her trews, 'I can't miss him in that outfit!'

7

Haute Couture

The multi-coloured jacket with its velvet lapels was thrown on top of a rumpled heap of yellow and black trousers, plaid waistcoat, green sneakers and spotted cravat. The trimmings of the sixth Doctor were being discarded.

Flanked by hanging rows of garments, the Doctor was selecting a new outfit in the dressing room of his TARDIS.

Posing before a full-sized mirror, he donned an ankle-length French cutaway trench coat with fold-back corners, *circa* 1812, tweaked a strand of his straight hair into a kiss curl on his forehead, crowned it with a cocked hat, then struck the Napoleonic stance of one hand tucked inside the trench coat.

'Wonder why he always stood like this?'

'Who?' asked the tetchy Rani. She was a fractious spectator of the parade.

'Napoleon Bonaparte!' He strutted about, admiring his reflection in the mirror. 'I think not. Lacks my natural humility.'

The Rani's raised eyebrows showed what she thought of that evaluation of his character!

Forsaking the Napoleonic gear, the Doctor plonked a capacious furry busby on his head. Swallowing him, it came down below his nose.

'No, doesn't look right without a horse.' His voice, muffled by the enveloping busby, made the bland statement even more ludicrous!

Dumping it, he ferreted among the racks, muttering encouragement to himself. 'Something dignified. Time Lordish.'

A mortar board and academic gown seemed to fit the bill. He promenaded rather grandly before the Rani.

'A little portentous perhaps, Mel.' He was hoping she'd contradict him.

She didn't. '*Pre*tentious is the word!'

Crestfallen, he flicked off the mortar board and, in rapid succession, tried on a variety of articles worn by the other six Doctors preceding him, culminating with the fifth Doctor's cricketing finery.

'This should bowl a maiden over,' he wisecracked.

The Rani was not amused.

Nor was she entranced by his ultimate apparel. A baggy, half-belted, cream jacket sagged wide to exhibit a pair of braces over a pullover decorated with question marks. From the collar of a tired shirt snaked a green and red paisley tie. Check trousers topped a pair of brown and white shoes.

'Ah, yes. Very *chic*,' he pronounced.

A squashed panama hat with upturned brim completed the sartorial mélange. 'A frowning man will clutch at a straw,' he quipped.

'Drowning –' the Rani began to correct, then changed her mind. 'Excellent. Very elegant,' she lied: anything to end this trifling exercise.

Tilting the flattened straw hat to a rakish angle, he surveyed the ensemble in the mirror.

'Thank goodness in this regneration I've regained my impeccable sense of haute couture!'

'If you've finished preening yourself, can we get what we came for?' No wheedling. Hard. This buffoonery had to be brought to a peremptory finale!

The Doctor studied her reflection in the mirror. Turned. Frowned. The biting tone evoked a sensation

44

of memory . . .

Superimposed on the Rani was another woman . . . Dressed identically . . . yet with a wide-eyed, elfin look . . .

The image fluctuated . . . to become the Rani . . . Then Mel again . . .

Wham! Realising his memory was trying to stage a recovery, the Rani had fetched him a resounding slap!

'What . . ? What . . ?'

'I'm sorry.' She wasn't. 'You seemed to be losing control.'

He rubbed his stinging cheek. 'I must have been hallucinating. I had an overwhelming sense of evil. And there was a name – Ra – Ral – Radi –'

'Radiation wave meter! That's what you came to the TARDIS to get.'

'Er – yes – did I? Now, let's see. Where d'you reckon I'd keep it?'

'Tool room.'

'Mmmm . . . Won't be a jiffy, Mel. Absence makes the nose grow longer.' He trotted out.

'Cretin!' She hurled the insult after him!

Alone, Mel paused. The steep incline she was climbing rose to a serrated ridge. The elements had eroded the granite into untidy obelisks which the imagination could transform into misbegotten effigies. Ruefully, Mel cast three of them as the witches in *Macbeth*.

A wistful smile relieved her gloomy speculation: if the Doctor were here, he'd quote Shakespeare's gory tragedy, that's for sure! She could herself. During schooldays in Pease Cottage, Sussex, England, she'd hammed her way through the role of the Third Witch.

Loneliness crowded in. Evocation of her lush and verdant birthplace brought home her predicament. She didn't even know where in the infinite universe she was

45

stranded.

Pluck, not self-pity, was Mel's style. She resumed the arduous climb. Maybe over the next horizon . . ?

A slight scuffling.

She turned . . . looked towards a clutter of boulders . . .

Nothing.

Imagination again. She clambered on.

. . . The sound of her scrunching footsteps carried to the boulders . . . a tawny, membraned claw crept over a craggy rim . . .

A tiny signal flickered on the Rani's mini-computer-bracelet as she waited for the Doctor in the TARDIS's control room.

Glancing furtively into the corridor to ensure the Doctor's continuing absence, she hurriedly took a reading from the bracelet and tapped the co-ordinates into the console.

A quartet of images came up on the screen, one of which contained the unsuspecting Mel . . .

'Yes, Urak?'

'We have found . . . the lost girl . . .' His use of the royal 'we' aggravated her, but the news he delivered was welcome.

'Focus in on her!'

Mel's section zoomed into close-up, filling the entire screen.

'Certainly . . . Mistress Rani . . .'

'Rani!' The Doctor bustled in.

There were powerful echoes here. Perplexed, he touched the controls. The familiar ambience was again inciting an inner conflict with the amnesia drug.

The Rani recognised the dilemma. 'Rani, Doctor?'

'Rani! Yes, that's the name. The evil name.'

'Is that her?'

46

He stared at the screen and Mel. 'Er – well – it must be – yes . . .'

'And she's evil?'

'Completely.' His fingers plucked frenetically at his pullover: he was unsure of himself; confused by her insidious manipulations.

'Then she must be destroyed.'

'Destroyed? Well – er – don't let's be hasty . . .'

A sharp click alerted Mel. She looked up.

A wispy, iridescent net was floating down towards her . . .

In reflex, she nipped aside!

The net fluttered to the gravel in a scintillating display of sparks . . .

Terrified, not understanding where the net came from or who had fired it, she dashed for freedom . . . and, inadvertently emulating the hapless Sarn, she blundered into a trip wire!

Her shin triggered the trap.

In a *whoosh* of dust and shale, a huge, opaque bubble with a bulging metal detonator encapsulated the screaming girl.

Steam spurted from its underside.

Mel frantically tore at the plastic.

To no avail.

The bubble began to spin.

Faster and faster.

Towards the edge of a cliff.

Mel kicked. She yelled. Tried to pierce the bubble with her fingernails. Attempted, by running counter-clockwise, to force it away from the precipice.

All in vain. The bubble rolled inexorably on, until, abandoning terra firma, it shot over the edge of the cliff . . .

8

Visions Of Greatness

When Mel had quit the drainage pipe against his better judgement, Ikona initially decided the girl could take her own chances. But playing the non-combatant was not in his nature.

Nor was appeasement.

The Rani's domination of Lakertya had been achieved with humiliating ease. His acquiescent countrymen, spoonfed by an indulgent regime, offered little opposition, preferring to believe the intrusion would be small-scale and transient.

A monumental mistake.

Anticipating this, Ikona tried to rally Beyus; the peace-loving intellectual rebuffed him, preaching non-aggression.

An innate dissident, Ikona then endeavoured to organise resistance groups. His efforts were fruitless.

Already nursing a burgeoning sense of disillusionment, he divorced himself from Lakertyan society and dwelt alone: an iconoclast living a hermit's existence.

Until Mel's intrusion. Her dogged defiance rekindled his dormant spirits. He could not abandon her to the bestial Tetraps.

Over the edge of the cliff and out into space soared the 'bubble', ready to drop and explode on impact!

It dropped.

But not onto hard ground. The perpendicular cliffs were bordering a lake . . . and the 'bubble's' landing was cushioned by the placid water.

Respite for Mel?

No. The deady sphere skittered across the surface towards the shore, on a bearing that meant the detonator would thump into the bank.

Undaunted, the resourceful girl again ran inside, trying to rotate the percussion cap out of harm's way. A brave effort that merely resulted in her losing balance.

Disaster seemed inevitable. She knew what to expect. Her cremation would be no less cruel than that of the female Lakertyan. If the Doctor had been in the vicinity, he might conceivably have been able to rescue her. Without him, there was nobody to come to her aid.

Belatedly reaching the cliff top, Ikona saw Mel's plight. Pell-mell, running a scree, he plunged into the lake and grappled with the bubble.

Killing its impetus, he contrived to steer it onto the beach.

Cautioning Mel to keep absolutely still, saturated, hissing with tension, he eased a bolt bonding the tumour-shaped mine to the plastic shell.

'Have you –' Mel's voice shattered his brittle concentration.

He glared at her.

She persisted, although less loudly. 'Have you done this before?'

'It's the first time! And, Mel, if you don't stop squawking it'll undoubtedly be the last!' Should the mine blow, he knew they would both be incinerated.

Steeling himself, he commenced twisting the bolt . . .

An explosive arc of fire crackled and leapt the gap of a megavolt catalyst as the Doctor toiled in the interior of the damaged machine.

'I can't help feeling sorry for the Rani, Mel. Though that bubble was a typically ingenious trap.'

Having seen the plastic 'bubble' sail over the edge of the cliff, the Rani had switched off the screen and cajoled the Doctor back to the lab.

'Then the Rani's got nobody to blame but herself,' came the unsympathetic reply.

'I suppose so . . .' Such atrocities could never be justified in the Doctor's book – no matter how villainous the victim may have been. 'But why was she prowling around on Lakertya?'

'I should've thought the answer was obvious.'

He stopped, awaiting the explanation.

'You must be on the brink of a major discovery.'

'It'd have to be a cosmic breakthrough for a neuro-chemist of her stature to come storming the barricades!'

Reining in her impatience, the Rani persisted with the sophistry: anything to keep him working!

'All the more reason for you to press on! Get there first! You've repeatedly said that in the wrong hands, scientific knowledge can be dangerous, haven't you, Doctor?'

'What scientific knowledge?' He flapped his arms in frustration. 'What am I doing? If only I could re-member!'

'Get the machine operational and maybe we'll find the solution.'

'Don't be ridiculous! The machine won't show me what's behind those two locked doors, will it?'

Baffled, he glared at the arcade door and the panel of the spherical chamber. 'It won't restore my memory, will it!' Bad-temperedly, he plonked the radiation wave meter close to the catalyst. 'If the Rani's after my ex-periment, we must be playing with fire.'

'Forget her! She's finished! Destroyed!'

'Is she? Don't underestimate her. She's an abomination: a brilliant but sterile mind.' Sparks flew from the catalyst. 'There's not a spark of decency in her.'

'I'm overwhelmed.'

'You are, Mel?'

'Such superior diagnostic talents.'

'It's my forté.'

'What a pity they can't be concentrated on the machine!'

'You're putting the cart before the hearse, Mel.'

'Hearse? Hmmm. You've got death on the brain, Doctor.'

Ikona's hand trembled . . .

Delicately . . . gradually . . . he eased the bolt . . .

A jerk! And it was free.

With mercurial speed, he extracted the mine and lobbed it, discus fashion, into the lake.

The explosion sent a spectacular spout of steaming water spurting upwards into the air.

The pyrogenics alerted Urak . . . and one of his elliptical quadviews zeroed in on the tell-tale fountain of water . . .

'Can you squeeze through the gap?'

The removal of the mine had presented a breach in the plastic shell.

'I – I think I can.' Being tiny was not always an advantage, but in this situation it spelt the difference between life and death.

With the dexterity of an eel, Mel squirmed out.

'Quickly! The noise will have alerted the Tetraps!' said Ikona.

Fear is an invincible spur: together they decamped. In their haste, they failed to notice Mel's scarf had caught on the jagged hole.

The rippling water was becalmed. Once again its surface was dappled with the reflections of the cliffs . . .

Only now there was another reflection . . .

A partially-winged biped standing on the cliff's edge
. . .

All that could be seen of the Doctor were the soles of his
shoes. The rest of him was inside the machine.

Using the respite, the Rani activated the monitor
screen to show the space view of the planet and the
malevolent asteroid circling it. Punching up calculations, she contemplated them thoughtfully.

'And another thing,' came the Doctor's voice from
the bowels of the machine, 'why was the Rani dressed
like you?'

'Perhaps she's fashion-conscious.' The jibe was
uttered with indifference: her mind was grappling with
a more profound and substantive issue.

'No, she was disguised. Practising another of her
talents.'

'Really?' She switched off the monitor. 'Are you
going to be much longer in there?'

''Fraid so. More *hasta* less *vista*.'

Not appreciating his humour, but assured of his
preoccupation, she printed two words on a small card
and, crossing to the arcade, tapped a combination into
the lock.

Careful not to alert the Doctor, she entered the arcade and quietly closed the door.

There was nothing furtive about her actions as she
approached the row of cabinets. 'Beyus!' she called.

His height emphasised by the thick tuft of hair arcing
from his scalp, Beyus appeared at the far end.

'Where were you?' she demanded.

'I was about to feed the Tetraps,' he replied, hooking
the pails of plasma onto the yoke.

Any resentment at being treated as a lackey was
suppressed: Beyus had to portray compliance. His

priority was to avoid antagonising the Rani. The defection of Sarn had apparently gone unnoticed. The longer that was so, the greater the prospects of her survival.

And yet he could not rid himself of a presentiment of ill-fortune. Why hadn't the Rani commented on the young Lakertyan's absence?

'When you've done that, I want you to prepare the empty cabinet.'

He nodded and left.

Those who deduced the Rani was devoid of feeling were wrong. Passing the cabinets, she experienced an intoxicating glow of satisfaction: Charles Darwin, Louis Pasteur, Albert Einstein, the *crème de la crème*! Adrenalin pumped through the Time Lady's veins and she saw, with unflawed clarity, the inspired beauty of the new dawn her scheme would usher in. Not only for this insignificant cosmic fragment called Lakertya, but for the whole of creation.

She halted by the vacant cabinet. A small smile embellished her lips. Soon the final piece of the mosaic would be in place. She slid the card into the empty slot and read again the name she had inscribed:

The Doctor

9

Face To Face

The powdery sand of the beach bore the imprint of
Mel's and Ikona's tracks. For the stalking Urak it
served as a conspicuous guide.

Mel's scarf was now clasped in his downy paw: a
fluttering trophy plucked from the 'bubble'.

Racing across uneven and pitted ground, the breathless
duo slithered into a crater.

Circumspect, gulping air, Ikona shuffled to the rim.

'Any sign of the – what did you call it?' asked Mel.

'A Tetrap.'

'What's it look like? All I saw was a net.'

'If you'd been close enough to see the hideous brute
it'd probably be the last thing you ever saw. Those nets
can stun or kill.'

'A pleasant thought.'

'Then let's go!' Ikona scrambled from the crater.

'Hold on! Hold on! Do you have a name?'

'Ikona.'

'Right. I'm grateful for your help, Ikona, but
gratitude isn't going to turn me into a puppet.'

'I've already come to that painful conclusion!'

'Then tell me, are we just running scared, or are we
heading somewhere in particular?'

'The answer to both questions is yes. Now, can we
go!'

Their goal was a rock face laced with vines. Un-
erringly Ikona flicked a vine, disentangling it. Like the

hideaway in the drainage pipe, this was another of his secret caches.

'You're full of surprises.'

'It's known as survival.'

Using the vine, he scaled the rock face. 'I'm not prepared to be completely supine. Unlike most Lakertyans. Now! Wait there!'

Resentment of Ikona's abrasive manner did not prevent Mel immediately regretting the loss of his reassuring presence. The many granite outcrops could offer concealment for a marauding Tetrap.

She glanced up to where Ikona was lodged precariously on a ledge. He delved into a fissure, extracting what appeared to be a firework. Tucking this into his belt, he again foraged in the inaccessible cave.

A soft scraping sound . . .

Distant. But not imaginary . . .

'Hurry, Ikona!' whispered Mel, fidgety with anxiety. 'Hurry!' Her skin was prickled with goose-pimples. A sixth sense warned her of imminent danger.

Urak's scrawny, membraned claw, sporting its pink, chiffon scarf, inched over a crenellated boulder . . .

Four elliptical screens converged into one . . .

Two hairy feet leapt into the air – and landed behind Mel.

She turned!

The vulpine, rodent-like face was covered with a gangrenous, oily down. Splayed, moist nostrils and thin sucking lips were dominated by a single luminous eye that glared unblinkingly from beneath a cockscomb of bristle. The veined, bloodshot orb had an enlarged pupil with a green halo.

As if this did not create an ugly enough apparition, above each delicately pointed pink ear, a similar eye bulged.

A fourth eye adorned the back of the Tetrap's skull.

These four eyes were the reason for the three hundred and sixty degree perspective: the quadview.

A predatory grimace exposed razor-sharp cuspids as the repulsive half-ape-half-rat leered at Mel. Then a venomous forked tongue spat at her!

Her scream was shrill enough to splinter glass! A rapid series of sharp retorts came from above.

Fireworks split asunder . . . and the air became festooned with shimmering strips of foil.

Urak threw up his arms, vainly trying to shield all four eyes.

'Mel! Up here!'

A hanging vine slapped against her shoulder.

Confused by the torrent of foil disorientating Urak, Mel did not budge.

'Grab the vine!'

She grabbed.

Ikona hauled feverishly . . . until Mel was able to clamber untidily into the fissure.

The foil strips that wrought havoc with the bat-like radar of the Tetrap optics, were beginning to settle.

Some clung to the greasy pelt covering of Urak's jutting, angular, full-bellied torso.

From above the elbows, a mucous membrane connected the spindly arms to the trunk in the fashion of a cape. The upper legs were bulky haunches that exuded a sinewy power.

Spitting venom, Urak glowered up to where his victims should have been stranded.

But they had vanished.

10

A Kangaroo Never Forgets

'I can't understand how I could make such a fundamental mistake!'

The numerals shown on the radiation wave meter
confounded the Doctor.

With almost demented fervour, he attempted to rip
the damaged casing off the machine.

'Let me.' Jostling him aside, the Rani unclipped the
casing without difficulty.

'What was the mistake?'

'You saw. The heat radiation from the catalyst was of
high frequency.'

'I – er – you used the wrong heat conducting
material?' Almost a slip! Had he noticed?

He hadn't. 'Yes.' Inspecting the casing. 'So
elementary. I broke the Second Law of Thermodynamics.'

'If we substituted a suitable material – would it
work?'

'You should be able to answer that, Mel. Didn't C. P.
Snow expound on thermodynamics?'

C. P. Snow was a man of letters whose lectures on the
Twin Cultures were world-famous on Earth. Mel would
have recognised the reference.

'Doctor, is this relevant?'

Carelessly discarding the casing, the Doctor prowled
the lab . . . but did not change his theme. 'You told me
you admired his writings. Read all his books.'

'I've obviously forgotten.'

The remark stopped him in his tracks.

'Forgotten, Mel? You? A kangaroo never forgets.'

'Elephant!' The automatic reply inaugurated a chain of thought the Rani had not intended.

'That's it! Memory like an elephant. A running gag . . . applied to you, Mel . . . I feel sure.'

Quite true. During the Doctor's and Mel's encounter with the terrifying Vervoids aboard the spaceliner *Hyperion III* in a previous adventure, he had, on several occasions, compared Mel to an elephant.

The Rani had to divorce him from such introspection!

'Perhaps the machine's blowing up affected my memory too. What were the readings?'

He shoved the radiation wave meter at her. 'Take it. Read for yourself.'

Crossing to the monitor, she fed in the information.

The Doctor had other ideas. Scavenging in the debris of his repair efforts, he cannibalised a T-joint and a length of thin rubber tubing. Cutting the tubing with his penknife, he fitted the pieces into the T-joint. He now had a three-ended tube.

Into one end he inserted a glass funnel. The other two ends he stuffed into his ears – an improvised stethoscope.

With dedicated interest, he tested his own hearts . . . satisfied, he then marched to the spherical chamber and pressed the funnel against its panel.

An almost ear-splitting throbbing, similar in rhythm to a pulsebeat accosted him . . .

What could that spherical chamber contain?

The exterior of the laboratory complex offered no clue to the Doctor's question either.

'That's where they've set up operations.' Ikona had led Mel to a vantage point above the headquarters.

The project robbed Mel of her propensity to verbalise her reactions.

A structure consisting of a bizarre mixture of styles nestled in a hollow. The main building was a tasteful architecture of marble, vaulted columns framing panels of pastel yellow, green and orange, all surmounted by a gracefully-proportioned pyramidal roof.

But Mel's awestruck silence derived from the desecration that had been inflicted on the harmonious edifice. The gaunt girders of a utilitarian ramp for a rocket, thrust through a rent that violated the pyramidal roof.

'Then that's where the Doctor will be,' pronounced Mel hoarsely, her throat dry.

'You can't be sure.'

'I can! You don't know the Doctor.'

'If he is in there – I probably never will!'

'There's no "if" about it. He's in there!'

'Well, the argument's academic. You won't gain access. The place is too well guarded.'

'Any notion what that rocket's for?'

'All I know is that building it cost the lives of many Lakertyans.' Not relishing the recollection, Ikona moved on.

'Something must have gone desperately wrong.'

'The logic of that misses me.'

'They kidnapped the Doctor,' explained Mel, tagging along beside him. 'No one would do that unless they were desperate for his help. He's not exactly pre-dictable!'

How the Rani would have applauded that sentiment!

'Would phb or pes do?'

No response.

She turned from evaluating the equations on the monitor. The Doctor had his improvised stethoscope

61

pressed against the curved panel.

Furious, she yanked the rubber tubing from his ears!

'What? What?'

'I asked you a question!'

'You did?' He indicated the spherical chamber. 'Mel. There's something in there!'

'No doubt.' Curt: subject terminated. 'Would phb or pes do?'

He frowned his lack of comprehension. Not that he didn't understand; polyhydroxybutyrat and polyether-sulphone were types of high grade plastic needed if the heat the machine would generate was to be conducted into the atmosphere and dissipated.

'As a substitute material for the machine casing!'

The penny dropped. 'Oh . . . yes – I'd prefer the phb. It's biodegradable. Don't want to litter Lakertya with non-destructible waste like they're doing on your planet, Mel.'

The preservationist homily accompanied an erratic search of shelves and drawers.

'What're you looking for?'

'Sugar and starch. We could ferment our own.'

'You won't find them here.' As a chemist, the Rani knew the process was quite practicable, but the delay would be unacceptable. 'What about the alternative?'

'Pes? That's hopeless. Petroleum-based plastic.'

'Slightly amber? Almost transparent?'

'Yes.'

She slammed shut the cupboard he was rummaging in. 'I know where there is some.'

He blinked at her in astonishment. 'Where?'

'Oh – a storeroom.'

'What storeroom?'

'In the grounds.'

'Whose is it?'

'A Lakertyan's, I assume.' Authoritatively. 'You

carry on here while I get the plastic.'

He picked up the acetylene torch. Hesitated. 'A Lakertyan's? I thought you said they weren't very advanced.'

'Did I?'

'Yes. When we discovered that skeleton.'

A dismissive shrug and she made for the exit to the grounds . . .

. . . At that precise moment, Mel was also approaching the grounds enclosing the lab.

After leaving the heights from which they had been contemplating the complex, Mel and Ikona's route took them towards the path where Sarn's sad skeleton lay.

Suddenly, Ikona bustled Mel behind a boulder. 'Stay put!'

Vouchsafing no explanation, he stepped onto the path and hurriedly intercepted a regal, handsome female Lakertyan.

'Faroon,' he called.

In her middle years, Faroon, dressed in a voluminous apricot cloak, her blonde tresses gathered into the symbolic plaited band worn by all her race, smiled affectionately. 'I'm glad to see you, Ikona. Although I ought not to be.'

A pleasure that should have been mutual, but Ikona's was marred by the need to divert her from the skeleton. 'Does my sitting on the fence mean we can't still be friends?' he asked.

'I'm afraid it does, Ikona, when you cut yourself off from the rest of us and deliberately oppose Beyus's instructions.'

'I can't accept he's right to collaborate.'

'He's being held hostage. He has no choice. It is the only way Beyus can save us from destruction.'

'He didn't save *her*, did he?' Mel's blunt interjection

63

was made in Ikona's defence. But its impact was disastrous. Her reference was to the skeleton.

Faroon's first reaction was of disquiet at the sight of this alien so reminiscent of the Rani.

'She won't harm you, Faroon. She's not with the Tetraps.'

A reassurance that served only to allay her fear of Mel . . . but she had seen the skeleton.

'You said . . . "her"?'

'Yes,' affirmed Mel. 'She was running from something.'

'You saw what happened too, Ikona?'

No response. Mel wondered why.

'You're not usually reluctant to air your thoughts,' Faroon chided. His silence further aroused her misgivings.

He remained mute.

She addressed Mel. 'From which direction did she come –?'

Mel pointed towards the laboratory complex.

Faroon shuddered: the qualms engendered by Ikona's lack of response were being given substance.

'As though she was escaping from the Tetrap headquarters.' Mel could not know the significance of the information. Or the wound it would create.

Ikona did. And realised he could no longer spare Faroon. 'It was . . . Sarn.'

Unable to conceal her anguish, Faroon moved close to the skeleton. The fear welling within had been confirmed.

'Who was Sarn?' Mel whispered to Ikona.

'The daughter of Faroon and Beyus . . .'

Mel felt thoroughly chastened. Unwittingly she had been the bearer of dreadful news. 'I'm – so – sorry,' she said to Faroon. 'I didn't realise.'

Fighting tears, the genteel Faroon expressed no

64

malice. 'I – I had to be – told . . .'

Ikona put his hand on her trembling arm. 'There was nothing that could be done, Faroon,' he added tenderly. 'She stepped on a trap.'

'Yet another victim!' Bitterness underscored her grief. 'I must go to Beyus . . .' This she could do because, alone of all her people, Faroon was permitted into the laboratory complex. From a pre-eminent position of consort to Beyus, she had been reduced to the role of go-between, conveying the Rani's pitiless decrees to the humbled populace whose idyllic existence had been transformed into a nightmare.

However, it was the loss of her daughter, not the blight plaguing Lakertya, that afflicted Faroon as she hurried away.

Permitting Faroon to get some distance ahead, Mel set off to follow.

'Where do you think you're going?' Ikona's manner was brusque.

'If Beyus is collaborating, he must be in the Tetrap headquarters.'

'He is.'

'And I've told you before, that's where I suspect the Doctor will be.'

A perceptive deduction.

One that led only to the next formidable hurdle.

Recognising Faroon, Urak had allowed her access, a facility he certainly would not grant Mel!

She and Ikona were concealed by an escarpment.

'You're still determined to get in?'

'No matter what the risk,' declared Mel pugnaciously.

'Madness!'

Mel shrugged: she couldn't see she had any alternative.

65

'It must be contagious,' muttered Ikona. 'I'll draw the Tetrap off . . .'

Deliberately revealing his presence, Ikona skirted the perimeter.

Urak's orders were to keep the area secure, but the prospect of catching the dissident Ikona was irresistible . . .

The ruse enabled Mel to gain entry to the grounds.

That was how she came to be weaving her way between the haphazard outcrops of rocks when the Rani was also weaving her way through the boulder-strewn grounds.

Ikona proved too swift for the lumbering Urak . . . but, in any case, his rear-view eye had glimpsed a more alluring prize – a generous mop of red curls bobbing along behind a granite ridge!

The missing girl!

Baring gleaming cuspids, Urak levelled his net-gun and fired!

Caught unawares, the victim was snared in a dazzling display of static . . .

11

When Strangers Meet

Dumping the acetylene torch on the bench, the Doctor, surveying the whole range of mysterious apparatus, reversed towards the exit.

Simultaneously, a pink and white garbed woman with curly red hair backed into the lab.

They bumped.

Spun about.

Stared at each other.

'Who are you?' she said.

'You!' he exclaimed.

Warily they circled.

'Where's Mel?'

'Where's the Doctor?'

'What've you done with her?' Belligerently, he lunged at her.

But she ducked beneath his outstretched arms, snatched up the acetylene torch and flourished it menacingly. A threat made comical by its weak flame.

Sneering, he advanced.

Hastily she increased the gas flow, forcing him into an undignified withdrawal from the spurting tongue of flame.

'Now we'll get the truth!' she declared.

He grabbed a stool to fend her off. But the seat cover caught fire!

He dropped the blistering stool and retreated in disarray.

'Where's the Doctor, you brute?'

'Here!'

'Where? Under the carpet?'

'There isn't any carp – *Me*, you stupid woman! *Me!*'

'Never! You're nothing like him! If the Doctor's been harmed, I'll –'

'Quit the melodramatics! Your pathetic impersonation doesn't fool me. Incidentally, that wig's not you at all.'

'You should talk! The Doctor's no oil painting but you'd frighten the cat! Oh –' A stab with the acetylene torch was brought to an abrupt halt! The rubber tubing was fully extended!

'I knew you weren't finished, Rani. I told Mel as much.'

'You told me?'

'Not you. *Mel!*' Circling again, out of range, a stratagem in mind.

'I *am* Mel. Who's the Rani?'

'Try looking in the mirror. The face of evil.'

'I've had enough of this drivel. Either you come clean or I'll burn the place down.'

The threat was made risible by the Doctor. With a Kung Fu yell, he sprang onto the bench and stamped on the acetylene torch's tubing.

The flame drooped to a puny flicker. Spluttered. Then died.

He leapt to the floor. The spritely Mel evaded him, putting the bench between them.

Impasse.

'All right, a compromise,' he panted. 'Let me feel your pulse.'

'Don't touch me!'

'Aha! The proof of the pumpkin's in the squeezing.'

'You don't even talk like the Doctor, you miserable fraud!'

'Come along let's feel your pulse – pulses! One for

each heart!'

'You're a raving lunatic!'

'Yes, perhaps I am. If you're the Rani, I'm flirting with destruction.'

'And if I'm Mel?'

'Mel? The worst she'd do is give me carrot juice.' He paused. Perplexed. 'Carrot juice . . . what made me say that?'

What made him say it was a twanging chord of memory. Mel, besides being a fitness buff, was also a nutritionist. Not only had she been insisting on fining down the rotund sixth Doctor, she had been determined to wean him away from sticky buns, chocolates and fattening milk shakes. Crisp lettuce, bean salad and carrot juice were to be the main ingredients of his staple diet.

He hated them. Especially the carrots.

'Perhaps the real Doctor told you,' she said, deliberately testing him. 'It was his favourite drink.'

'Favourite? I hate carrot juice!'

'Oh?' Doubt coloured conviction.

'Aha! Caught you out, didn't I?'

'If you're the Doctor . . .' Was she beginning to waver? 'Why do you look like that?'

'I've regenerated. And I'm suffering from post-regeneration amnesia. At least, that's what I thought . . .'

He rubbed the injection mark on his wrist.

'Exchange is no mockery: you feel my pulse. Go on. You want proof I'm a Time Lord.'

Mel's scepticism persisted. She kept her distance.

'Look, I'll lean across the workbench with my other hand behind my back.'

Jigsaw puzzles intrigued Mel when she was a child. Were the pieces of this jigsaw melding together? Regeneration. Carrot juice. His willingness to let her feel his pulse – well, pulses . . .

Charily, she accepted the offer: 'A double pulse! You really are the Doctor!'

'That's what I've been telling you! Yours now.'

She loosened the tight, candy-striped cuff of her blouse. 'I knew about regeneration, of course. I was with you at your trial.' There she had met the Valeyard, a future regeneration of the Doctor.

Failing to locate a second pulse, the Doctor patted her hand. Pieces of his jigsaw puzzle were fitting together too. The impersonation. The identical clothes. The drug which he felt certain accounted for the small puncture in his skin. Accounted for the memory loss too.

'But . . . you're nothing like you were. Face. Size. Hair. Everything's changed.'

'Become more of a fool, too, it seems, Mel. Doesn't bode well for my seventh persona, does it? Being so completely taken in by that devious Rani.'

Red wig askew, the Rani lay on the ground, her arm enmeshed in Urak's net.

Casually, he kicked the arm aside to release his net! The callous jolt prompted her into recovery.

Immediately, his attitude altered. 'I am sorry . . . Mistress, I had . . . not seen you . . . dressed in those . . . clothes before . . .'

'Inquests bore me!' the Rani snapped, striding towards her TARDIS. This was in the shape of a pyramid: the efficient chameleon circuit had adapted the exterior to blend perfectly with its environs.

Urak dogged the Rani.

'Where d'you think you're going?'

'With you, Mistress . . .'

'I've told you not to enter my TARDIS without permission! Stay here!'

70

Depicted on the monitor screen was the planet and its orbiting satellite.

'Is that Lakertya?' Mel asked.

'Yes . . . but it's the asteroid of Strange Matter that bothers me.'

'Strange Matter? Never heard of it.'

'You should have, Mel. A Princetown physicist discovered it in the Earth year 1984.'

'Computers are my speciality, not nuclear physics.'

'It's an incredibly dense form of matter. A lump the size of this bench would weigh more than your Earth.'

'Well, what can the Rani's interest be?'

'An astute question. If that asteroid exploded, it would send out a blast of gamma rays equivalent to a supernova!'

'Then it'd be goodbye Lakertya.'

'With everything else in this part of the galaxy. When the Rani dabbles, she dabbles on a grand scale.'

While talking, he prowled the lab. The spherical chamber proved an irresistible magnet. 'Listen,' he said to Mel, stuffing his ear against the panel.

'Weird,' Mel replied, listening. 'Like a giant heartbeat.'

He strode across the room, rapping the catalyst machine and the crystal tank. 'Why, Mel, why? What's she up to?' A tattoo of frustrated thumps on the arcade door. 'It begins in there!'

The rat-a-tat-tat on the arcade door startled Beyus who was comforting Faroon.

'Forget it, Doctor. Let's hightail it out of here to the TARDIS,' came Mel's voice.

'What! Abandon these Lakertyans to the Rani's machinations? Impossible!'

Beyus, his stoicism strained to the limit by the

71

sombre news Faroon had imparted, walked slowly to the door . . .

'Given time, I could work out the combination,' the Doctor chuntered, fiddling with the lock.

Watching him, any lingering doubts Mel had were banished: a physical transformation may have taken place with the regeneration, but the quintessence of the crusading maverick was unimpaired.

A sigh. 'I suppose I'll have to break in –'

'Nine – five – three,' came Beyus's voice from beyond the door.

'Did you hear a voice, Mel? Or am I hallucinating?'

'Go on, Doctor! Nine – five – three!'

'Who'd've thought she'd've been so obvious? That's my age' – tapping in the numbers – 'and the Rani's!'

The Rani had lied to the Doctor about seeing the polyethersulphone in a Lakertyan's storeroom. There was only one place where such sophisticated material would be housed: the repair bay in her TARDIS.

She riffled through a miscellaneous collection of plastic sheets, selected the appropriate piece and, using a laser beam cutter, reduced it to the correct measurements for the casing of the machine.

Leaving the TARDIS, she found Urak faithfully waiting outside.

'May I assist . . . you, Mistress . . ?'

'That girl's on the loose in the grounds. Find her before she finds the Doctor.'

'Yes, Mistress . . .'

Urak loped off.

The Rani made for the complex . . . where Mel and the Doctor were discovering the iniquitous secret of the arcade.

12

'You Know, Don't You!'

'Charles Darwin . . . Za Panato . . . Louis Pasteur . . . Albert Einstein,' recited Mel, reading the labels on the cabinets.

'Names which mean nothing to us,' said Beyus.

'Geniuses. Every one of them. The Rani's brought together the most creative minds and the most powerful matter in the universe. The scope of her imagination is breathtaking,' stated the Doctor.

'You sound as though you admire her.' The anguish from his daughter's death gave Beyus's reproof a tinge of bitterness.

'A murderess,' cried Faroon. 'Sarn was not her first victim. There have been many.'

'Not admiration,' apologised the Doctor. 'Fascination. And sadness. If only the Rani could have directed her exceptional talents for good!'

'The fascination's mutual,' called Mel, indicating the label on the vacant cabinet. 'She's reserved this for you!'

A rare moment: the Doctor's resilience stayed in neutral! He gulped, then tried, unconvincingly, to shrug off the panic he felt.

'What –' He moistened his lips. 'What is it I can contribute that these other geniuses can't?'

Accompanied by Mel, Faroon and Beyus, he beat a retreat into the lab.

'You're a Time Lord,' suggested Mel.

'With a unique conceptual understanding of the

properties of time . . .'

Ignoring the planet and its asteroid flickering on the monitor screen, he made for the spherical chamber.

'Do you have any idea what's in there?' he asked Beyus.

Beyus was at the exit, keeping watch for the Rani. 'No. She's never permitted me to see.'

'Pity. Why have you – um – er – assisted?'

'Collaborated is the word you are avoiding. I've no choice – She's coming!'

Stampede!

In the general scramble, the Doctor bundled Mel into the arcade. 'Look after Mel!'

'I'll take her with me,' volunteered Faroon.

'Doctor, you can't stay!'

'Go, Mel! Go!'

Slamming the door to the arcade, he scampered to the machine, adopting a bravura show of non-chalance as the Rani entered.

Disaster! He had omitted to switch of the monitor!

'Let me see,' he blustered. 'Yes. Yes. That's poly-ethersulphone.' He took possession of the amber sheet as a diversion. 'Excellent. How clever of you, Mel. Where did you find it?'

'Storeroom,' came the flat reply. She had not missed the flickering screen. 'Why's the monitor on?'

'On? Is it? The monitor? I was just trying to jog my memory. No luck though. Hold the other end, Mel!'

She held the plastic sheet . . . but her keen eyes were not on the Doctor tightening the casing clips. They were on the scorched stool. 'Turned pyro-maniac, too, have you?'

'Pyro – er – yes. Soldering what-d'you-call-it slipped. You're not concentrating, Mel! Hold the sheet still. I'll have to manoeuvre it into position.'

'You're rather adept at manoeuvring, aren't you,

Doctor?'

A flutter of uncertainty from him. 'Ah well, where there's a will there's a Tom, Dick and Harry.' He fastened the last clip. 'QED.'

'Do I take it the machine's now operational?'

'No, no, no, no! There's information I simply must have before I make the final delicate adjustments.'

'Such as?'

'Ideally, what's in that spherical chamber.'

'Less ideally?'

'The identity of this rather interesting substance.' He dipped his knuckle into the goo in the crystal tank.

'The information's essential, is it?'

'Crucial.'

'So if I told you its chemical composition, I could do this –' She stabbed the starter button.

'Stop! You can't'

His voice was drowned by a composite din of gurgling, engine whine and staccato cracks from the catalyst as the simmering, glutinous liquid oozed through the elaborate arrangement of tubes and transparent pipes on its journey to the spherical chamber.

The Doctor's consternation held him spellbound.

The Rani watched him with cool appraisal.

'You know, don't you?' She stripped off the wig to release her own brunette tresses. 'But your usefulness is not over. You've another role to play!'

Wildly, the Doctor snatched up a mess of flex and cables, tossing it over the Rani. In the brief respite, he managed to tap the combination number into the lock and dashed into the arcade.

Neither Mel nor Faroon was there. The Doctor brushed past Beyus and made for the door at the far end of the narrow arcade.

'Not that way!'

75

Beyus's warning went unheeded.

The Doctor had dashed into the portal of the eyrie
. . . and nipped inside . . .

Not only the darkness confused him. Mote-infested
glimmers of light suggested the eyrie boasted no door
connecting with the outside. Nor did any cool fresh air
sweeten the fetid atmosphere that wafted in pungent
waves off the greasy brown pelts of the abominations
hanging upside-down from the rafters.

'Out of my path!' The Rani stormed past Beyus.

She, too, descended into the eyrie.

Squinting through the gloom, she knelt beside a
rack of net-guns to inspect the gap between the
hanging Tetraps and the floor.

There was no sign of the escapee's legs. Repulsed
by the stench, she withdrew.

A rustling from the rafters. But this was not from the
dreaming Tetraps.

It was the Doctor – suspended from the rafters!

Gingerly, he lowered himself, bringing his head
level with that of a sleeping Tetrap.

A veined eye snapped open!

A forked tongue darted between razor sharp
teeth . . .

13

Rendezvous With A Tetrap

'Er – excuse me – we may not see eye to eye –'

All four eyes opened, giving the Tetrap a quadview of the eyrie.

'Er – I mean – try to see it my way . . .'

The rear and side eyelids closed: the creature was focusing on its quarry.

'Oh dear – I'm really not intending to be personal . . .'

Oily pelt glistening in what little illumination shafted through the bars of the grating, the Tetrap insinuated itself between the Doctor and freedom.

'After all, a bat may look at a Time Lord . . .'

The slavering tongue flicked –

A click!

A spurt of white flame!

The Tetrap flopped to the ground beneath a sizzling electronic net.

'Quickly, Doctor!' It was Beyus.

Non-aggression was Beyus's philosophy and his avowed intent, but the Doctor had voluntarily championed their cause with no concern for his own life. Having waited for the Rani to go into the grounds, Beyus had descended to the eyrie and unhitched a net-gun.

'You must leave,' he urged.

The Doctor needed no second bidding.

'You will have to escape through the laboratory,' said Beyus, preceding the Doctor into the arcade. 'The Rani left by the other door.'

'Mistress Rani?'
Urak's voice.
From the lab!

'Mistrss Rani?'
Urak's sweeping quadview established the Rani
was not in the lab. She could be in the spherical
chamber. Or the arcade. Unfortunately for the Doctor,
Urak decided on the arcade.

Urak's hefty, hairy carcass blocked the doorway as
he perused the lengthy expanse.
The Rani was not there.
Nor was the Doctor.
Only Beyus checking the dials on the cabinets.
'You . . . Lakertyan . . . have you seen the . . .
Mistress Rani . . ?'
Beyus was slow to reply.
'Quickly . . ! Answer . . !'
'She went into the grounds.'
Urak stamped along the arcade. 'Clear my way . . !'
There was ample space for him to pass but he chose
to make Beyus squeeze into a niche. 'The Mistress
has . . . profound insight . . . but I think she . . . is
mistaken . . . to rely on . . . any of your . . . worthless
race . . .'
Failing to provoke a response, he continued on.
Pausing only for the Tetrap to disappear from sight,
Beyus unsealed the cabinet labelled *The Doctor* –
and its namesake eased forth!
'Can't say I share the Rani's taste in pets!'
'The Tetraps are nobody's pets.' Anticipation of the
Rani's return made Beyus nervous. 'And you'd be
wise not to forget it.'
'This is what I'll never forget!' Indignantly the
Doctor trudged the line of incarcerated luminaries.

'Unique talents! Every one of them! The Rani's roamed the universe plucking these geniuses out of time! At the height of their powers! Reducing them to the status of laboratory specimens!'

His rising, intemperate anger perturbed Beyus. 'Go! Please!'

'Time! The concept of time! I'm sure it's at the core of what she's up to. Why else reserve a place for me – a Time Lord – in this abysmal parade?'

'If you are still here when she comes back, you will find out. From inside that cabinet!'

'Which you'll help her put me in.'

There was just a slight hesitation before Beyus answered. 'If she catches you . . . yes.' So far and no further: compassion had prompted him to save this stranger, but expediency was motivating him now.

'You know, Beyus, your collaboration with the Rani is difficult to understand.'

'My people are under threat. If you do manage to escape, go to the Centre of Leisure. The reason is there.' He ushered the Doctor into the lab. 'Now, hurry! And be careful. The grounds outside are a minefield of traps.' He had already reached the exit.

'There's nothing outside to compare with that!' Fingers fluttering in vexation, the agitated Doctor was staring at the asteroid on the monitor screen.

'A harmless asteroid?'

'It's composed of Strange Matter, Beyus. A devastating force. With the right trigger' – his roving gaze switched to the gurgling liquid in the tank and to the pulsating machine – 'that harmless asteroid, as you call it, could incinerate your planet. And anything else in this corner of the galaxy!' Again the spherical chamber claimed his attention. He pressed his ear to the panel. 'What *has* she got imprisoned in there?' Frustrated by the lock, he slapped and kicked the solid panel in frustration.

It was almost as if the physical venting of his anger sent a dose of adrenalin to his brain. Inspiration dawned.

'Well, all good things come to a bend,' he misquoted.

Strutting to the catalyst machine, he wrenched off the plastic sheet, ripped a component from the innards and flourished it aloft. 'Microthermister.'

All activity in the apparatus had ceased.

'I doubt if she'll have a spare!'

'She won't need one. You are going to put it back!' Beyus snatched at the microthermister. Missed. 'Give it to me –' Another snatch – but the Doctor, in evading the bid, caused Beyus to fall, knocking his head against the dais.

'I'm sorry . . . I'd no intention of hurting you –'

The patter of high heels from the arcade!

Torn between wanting to minister to Beyus and the desire to flee with the microthermister, the Doctor wisely decided to afford priority to the latter.

He fled.

Desultory hiccuping slurps from the liquid in the crystal tank greeted the Rani.

'Who's sabotaged that?' she demanded, giving the dazed Beyus an unsympathetic shake. 'What happened?'

'I – I – my head –'

'Was it the Doctor?'

'I – do not know who he is. He stole something from the machine. I tried to stop him –'

The Rani stabbed a large red button on the control board.

A klaxon wailed.

The banshee blaring percolated to Ikona.

80

Lurking near the perimeter, he saw Faroon leaving the complex amidst the furore incited by the flashing red warning lights and persistent strident whine.

He wondered whether Mel was safe: perhaps this general alert was the result of her incursion.

Faroon had thought this too. True to her word, she had been conducting Mel through the grounds when she spotted the Rani, hands on hips, on a ridge scanning the surrounding area.

'She's looking for us,' said Faroon.

'Maybe,' replied Mel as they cringed behind a free-standing pyramid, unaware that it was the Rani's TARDIS! 'I can think of a more likely explanation – the Doctor's on the loose.'

Circumspectly, she peeked round the angle of the TARDIS. 'Whatever the reason, Faroon, you mustn't be caught with me.'

'I cannot abandon you. I promised.'

'I'll be all right. Really, I'll be fine!'

Faroon had reluctantly complied.

But Mel's confidence, boldly declared to Faroon, had evaporated with the onset of the klaxon: she needed a better haven.

Cautiously, she again craned her neck round the corner to spy out the land.

Moist nostrils quivering, a Tetrap glared un-blinkingly at her.

She opened her mouth to scream.

No sound came.

In abject terror, she turned to run. Urak confronted her!

Gloatingly he spread his bony, hairy arms, stretching the mucous membrane cape.

Mel, transfixed by fright, was enveloped into the embrace of the nightmarish apparition.

81

'The Mistress . . . will be over . . . joyed to see you . . .' With the tenderness of an obscene lover, Urak's lips drew closer to Mel's face.

The forked tongue darted, piercing her ashen cheek.

A scarlet glow emanated from Mel . . . When it faded, she was stiff. Paralysed. Only her wide, terror-stricken eyes had movement.

Urak released her to the guard.

'*Uoy wonk erehw . . . ot ekat reh!*' Translated from the Tetrapyriarban, his instruction was: 'You know where . . . to take her!'

14

The Centre Of Leisure

Flight, the fugitive Doctor decided, should not be a rash skedaddle. No, it should reject the obvious; he opted for a longer, more arduous route.

There was also an added bonus: the labyrinth of misshapen rocks provided excellent cover.

Or so he thought!

'Stop! Don't take another step!' came a warning.

'This is a turn-up for the cook!' exclaimed the Doctor. 'A talking rock!' For only an inanimate monolith confronted him.

Until Ikona's golden mane poked from behind it.

'You must be the Doctor!' A conclusion accompanied by a wry smile. 'I've met your companion, Mel.'

'Well, don't hold that against me.'

'I can see where she gets her sense of humour. And you're going to need it!'

'That bad?' The Doctor had stayed rooted to the spot.

'Move those stones. *Very gently!*'

The Doctor obeyed . . . glistening in the granulated shale was the percussion cap of a 'bubble'.

'More of the Rani's nasty tricks,' he said, retreating. 'If you've met Mel, you must be Ikona –'

Ikona had disappeared.

The Doctor soon discovered why: a Tetrap guard had stolen up on him!

'Er – haven't I seen you hanging around somewhere?' the Time Lord stuttered.

Confident of snaring the escapee, the Tetrap levelled its net-gun. A firework was lobbed high in the air . . . disintegrated!

Slivers of glittering foil cascaded onto the Tetrap, disorientating it. Blinded in all four eyes, the ungainly beast almost blundered into the Doctor.

Almost, but not quite – the spritely Time Lord nimbly stepped aside – and the Tetrap stumbled onto the exposed mine!

With a mighty *whoosh*, the 'bubble' encaspulated the Tetrap.

'I'm forever growing bubbles,' gasped the astounded Doctor.

'Come on!' urged Ikona. He knew the volatile sequence his firework had set in train. 'Behind here!'

The Doctor attained shelter fractionally before the 'bubble' detonated, obliterating the Tetrap guard.

'Where's Mel?' asked Ikona when the dust had settled.

He had to repeat the question: this Doctor, like all his predecessors, had an innate repugnance for violence.

'Doctor! Where's Mel?'

'Oh . . . Yes . . . Quite safe. She went with Faroon.'

Safe?

Paralysed by the venom from Urak's spitting tongue!

The fetid murk of the eyrie now had a solitary segment of brightness. White pants contrasting with the brown pelts of the dozing Tetraps, Mel's rigid form was hanging upside-down from the rafters.

Her eyes widened with revulsion as, next to her, a tawny membrane cape flapped while its owner dreamed a Tetrapian dream . . .

84

'Tell the Doctor he can have the girl in return for the microthermister he stole!'

The Rani, now dressed in her own scarlet clothes, was speaking to Faroon. She had been summoned to the arcade on the Rani's orders. Beyus was with her.

'Er – how will I find this Doctor?'

'You won't have to. He'll make contact with other Lakertyans, and try to stir up trouble.' A final injunction. 'And don't be taken in by his glib tongue.'

She flounced into the laboratory.

'Do as she says, Faroon.' Beyus sensed the reluctance in his consort. 'You know the price our people will pay if you disobey.'

Disobedience was not worrying Faroon. Beyus's welfare was.

'You would not try to escape as – as Sarn did?'

Beyus's reply was gentle. 'Faroon . . . I have obeyed all the Rani's commands. Carried out the most menial of tasks. When she is so near to completing her experiment, why would I now take such a risk?'

'What happens then? When her work is finished?'

'She will leave Lakertya.'

'Will she, Beyus?'

'That was her promise.'

'And when she does?'

'Our lives will return to normal.'

'Normal, Beyus? . . . Without Sarn . . ?'

Understanding her grief, sharing it, Beyus escorted her to the exit.

'Deliver the message to the Doctor, Faroon. I believe you will find him in the Centre of Leisure.'

Argumentative and resourceful was how Mel had described Ikona during her brief reunion with the Doctor.

Well, the Doctor would be eternally grateful for the

resourcefulness, but the verbal hassle was missing as the tall, young Lakertyan uncommunicatively led him across a brook.

Beyond the creek, carved into the sheer face of a towering mountain, was an intricate, abstract motif of pyramids. Although apparently at random, the composition conveyed a civilised harmony that contrasted vividly with the primordial landscape.

'Quite artistic,' said the Doctor encouragingly.

'We Lakertyans excel in decorative skills.' The trenchant irony did not invite discussion on local culture!

Several Lakertyans sauntered from an entrance tunnelled into the mountain.

'There's no restriction of movement then? Lakertyans can come and go freely?'

'Providing they obey the edicts of Beyus!' retorted Ikona. 'And don't try to get into the laboratory complex.'

Courteously and with an affable smile, the Doctor lifted his straw hat to a couple of Ikona's compatriots.

He was studiously ignored.

Disconcerted, he lingered.

Not Ikona. Unabashed by the lack of social graces, he continued into the Centre of Leisure.

Light twinkled and scintillated from the myriad polished surfaces of a huge, many-faceted globe. Suspended from the roof, it revolved like a mobile, its rhythm almost mesmeric.

Yet the globe was at odds with the dominant theme of the Centre, which appeared to have been designed by a devotee of cubism. A honeycomb of cubicles boxed in a plaza which encompassed a crystal clear pool. Fringing the pool, were terracotta statuettes decorated with ceramic silver fronds.

Gracefully-chiselled fish spouted fountains of water.

Many Lakertyans idly frequented the peaceful setting. Some occupied the cubicles, playing video and hologram games. Others, lounging on cushioned, swinging recliners, were immersed in strobic lights, listening to music through headphones.

Exotic frescos, plants and goblets of wine completed the hedonistic scene.

Strolling onto a gallery overlooking the plaza, Ikona paused until the Doctor joined him.

'Centre of Leisure!' Ikona declared sarcastically. 'Centre of Indolence!'

'Not a favourite haunt of yours, I gather, Ikona?'

'No.' He preceded the Doctor along the gallery. 'I can't imagine why Beyus told you to come to this place.'

'He said I'd find the answer to his subservience here.'

'From these spineless pleasure-seekers?'

'Why not?'

'It'd require effort, that's why. They've become spoon-fed drones. There's no need for them to strive. An indulgent system provides all!'

They descended a staircase.

'Didn't Beyus give you any clue what to look for?'

'He was too anxious for explanations.' The Doctor peered about. 'Whatever the threat, it must be considerable.'

Bathed in a languid peach glow, the Centre exuded tranquillity.

'Can you see anything that's different? New?'

'Only that!' Ikona indicated the globe. 'Another pointless embellishment.'

'Mmmm. I wonder . . . Let's ask.'

'We'll be interrupting their pleasure!' Despite his scepticism, Ikona ducked into the nearest cubicle.

'Can you tell me –?' The player shunned him!

In the next cubicle, the Lakertyan did not even wait for the question before rudely snubbing Ikona.

'I did warn you,' he said to the Doctor.

'There's none so deaf as those who clutch at straws.'

'If you say so.' Ikona placidly accepted the mixture of proverbs.

Then: 'Lanisha!' Ikona called, delight in his greeting.

The young male Lakertyan's response was ambiguous: pleasure tempered by discretion. Nevertheless, they exchanged the Lakertyan salutation of pressing right palms together.

'Lanisha, can you tell me what that globe is for?'

'We've been forbidden to have anything to do with you, Ikona.'

'You're going to ignore your own brother?'

'I obey the orders of Beyus.'

In abject contrast, Beyus was not issuing orders but receiving them; and in a manner which paid scant regard to the dignity of his rank.

'Answer the . . . Mistress Rani . . .' croaked Urak contemptuously. He had found the burnt remains of the cremated Tetrap guard. He had also found the foil strips that he was thrusting at Beyus.

'Do you recognise these?' the Rani repeated her question.

Before replying, Beyus fingered the red and gold torque draped from his shoulder. The torque was matched by a chain of red and gold beads. Both were symbols of high office.

'The foil strips are from the fireworks we used at our carnivals.' His use of the past tense was significant: carnivals and fiestas, an integral adjunct of Lakertyan

88

ceremonial, had been prohibited by the Rani.

'This was fired at no carnival,' she reprimanded. 'It was used to enable the Doctor to escape.'

'Causing the . . . death of a . . . Tetrap . . .'

The Rani coded instructions into the monitor.

A graphic of the multi-faceted globe began to assemble on the screen.

'None of my followers would be responsible!' Beyus's consternation was heightened by Urak's snuffle of unadulterated bliss as the graphic took shape.

'You're careful not to deny it's the work of a Lakertyan.'

'You can't do this! It will be punishing the innocent!'

'Guilt by association. I warned you of the consequences of subversion.' She pressed a button on her mini-computer-bracelet . . .

The globe stopped revolving.

A hush filtered through the Centre of Leisure . . . to be broken by an angry, wasp-like buzzing.

Panic!

Game-players burst from their cubicles.

Loungers tumbled from their cushioned hammocks.

Shouts of terror blotted out the music.

All stampeded for the exit!

Ikona and the Doctor, not privy to the horror that was about to beset the Centre's occupants, were the only stationary figures.

Not for long.

The vengeance of the Rani would recognise no exceptions . . .

The buzzing intensified as a facet of the globe opened and four mutated hornets flew out.

In rapid succession, three of the hornets dived on

three screaming Lakertyans.

A piercing sting. And the buzzing ceased.

So did the screams of the victims.

Recipient and donor died instantly: equal sufferers in the Rani's scheme of submission.

The Doctor and Ikona stood transfixed – until the fourth killer insect buzzed perilously close . . .

Galvanised by fear, they raced for the staircase.

The hornet kept pace!

Drew ahead.

Settled on top of a curtain and increased its buzzing preparatory to a final dive.

Cut off from the exit, Ikona and the Doctor presented choice targets.

But the insect swooped behind the curtain.

The buzzing climaxed.

Slowly the curtains parted – and Lanisha slumped to the gallery floor . . .

Ikona, dropping to his knees beside the body of his brother, was reproached by biting words.

'Do you still insist Beyus should not count the cost of resistance, Ikona!' Faroon had arrived from the laboratory complex just as the four hornets had been launched. 'If every cell in the globe were opened, there would not be a Lakertyan left alive!'

The Doctor's puckish face wore a grim expression as he considered Faroon's words. Only too well did he understand Beyus's servile acceptance of the Rani's subjugation.

'Doctor,' Faroon interrupted his reverie. 'I have a message for you. It concerns your companion, Melanie . . .'

90

15

Exchange Is A Robbery

The plateau, a grey flatness relieved occasionally by
whirlygigs of sand from capricious wind eddies, was
the chosen venue for the exchange.

With Mel beside him, Urak stomped and snorted
impatiently. None of his elliptical quadviews showed
the adversaries with whom he had been sent to
barter. Not that he would have accepted the con-
ditions for the recovery of the microthermister. The
Mistress Rani might believe this feckless Doctor was
honourable, but what if the Time Lord was not
afflicted by such a weakness? There could easily be
an attempt to rescue the girl without returning the
stolen component.

A straw hat topped a rise at the far rim of the
plateau.

Urak snuffled.

The straw hat was lifted and waved.

Mel waved vigorously back.

'Let Mel come towards me!' shouted the Doctor. 'I'll
keep my side of the bargain. You'll get what you
want.' He was not prepared to trust the Rani let alone
this monstrosity whose origins and antecedents he
had yet to discover: suffice it that the Tetrap was the
Rani's acolyte and, therefore, tarred with her brush!

He saw the grotesque, snouted head nod and Mel
start forward.

She passed, without recognition, the camouflaged
drainage pipe.

'Now, Ikona! Now!' yelled the Doctor.

Levering himself from the pipe, Ikona placed the microthermister on the sand and sprinted after Mel. He wanted to keep a fair distance between himself and the possible range of the net-gun.

Netting the enemy was not on Urak's agenda. Pleasing the Rani was. Collecting the microthermister, he waited until Mel had almost reached the Doctor.

'So stupid . . .' he cackled, exposing pointed fangs in derision. 'You are not . . . a worthy . . . opponent . . . for the Rani . . .'

'What's he crowing about, Mel?' The question ended falteringly.

Mel walked straight through him like a ghost!

The Doctor had been hoodwinked.

'What happened? Where's Mel?' asked Ikona. 'I saw her . . . and then she vanished!'

'It was a hologram of Mel.' A hologram is a three-dimensional image recreated by light manipulation so that the spectator is deceived into believing the image is a solid object.

'A hologram!' reiterated the Doctor, gazing balefully at the receding hulk of Urak. 'As substantial as the Rani's scruples!'

The substance, not the shadow, was being unhooked from the rafters in the eyrie.

Rigid, wide-eyed with fear and shouldered by a Tetrap guard, Mel was borne from the subterranean lair.

'As soon as the machine's operational, increase the brain stimulation.'

The Rani was speaking to Beyus. Having re-inserted the microthermister, she was in the arcade checking the cabinets before re-activating the machines.

'But that would take them past the danger level,' said Beyus, concerned for the incarcerated geniuses.

'I'm in danger of missing the Solstice – which is far more critical!'

'The computer controls will need constant supervision. I can't manage alone.'

The eyrie grating clanged and the lumbering Tetrap carried the petrified Mel up into the arcade.

'So I've anticipated,' the Rani retorted. 'I've got just the expert for you.'

She snapped a capsule under Mel's nose.

Immediately a revitalising fit of ague quivered through the girl's paralysed limbs.

'Beyus, she's your responsibility.'

'Mine? How can I govern her behaviour? She's not Lakertyan.'

'Just make sure she understands the penalty of non-cooperation!'

Penalty or not, Ikona and the Doctor were re-entering the lists.

'In my opinion, returning to the laboratory is a futile exercise. I've a feeling Mel's beyond all help.'

'No, the Rani wouldn't do that. She never does anything without a reason!' The Doctor was adamant.

Ikona glanced at the slight figure manfully negotiating the precarious track. Already he could detect beneath the vulnerability an obdurate courage to be reckoned with.

'Then why the elaborate deception? Why didn't she just release Mel?'

'A bird in the hand keeps the Doctor away.'

'You're probably right.' Again the placid acceptance of the mixed-up proverb.

'Only in this case, Ikona, it'll have the opposite result!'

A staccato crack from the catalyst.

A gurgling from the viscous sludge in the crystal tank.

The pyramid machines were functioning.

Nevertheless, the Rani was discontent. 'The increase in brain activity is not enough! We're going to miss the Solstice!'

Scrutinising the space view of Lakertya on the screen, she simultaneously punched in calculations.

'Perhaps the . . . stimulation . . . of a greater . . . genius, Mistress . . . a brilliance . . . that surpasses . . . all others . . .'

Urak's fawning idolatry produced a cold response. 'Do I gather you're suggesting *I* climb into one of those cabinets?'

'Your capable . . . presence is . . . squandered in here . . . I could . . . operate the machines . . .'

The plausible explanation foundered. 'I'm sure you could.' She went into the arcade.

'Prepare the Doctor's cabinet for occupation,' the Rani instructed Beyus.

'That'll be a waste of effort!' Mel retorted. 'You've got to find him first. And then catch him!'

Her recalcitrance worried Beyus. It merely spurred the Rani.

'I need neither find nor catch him,' she declared, a small smile emphasising her smugness. 'The bumbling fool is ready-made as a sacrificial lamb.'

'He's shrewder than you think! Underestimating the Doctor's a common fault!'

'Really?'

The condescension goaded Mel. 'He's got

qualities you'll never have!'

'Such as?'

'Something I'd call humanity.' Even to Mel the answer sounded lame.

'You're as sentimental as he is.' The disparagement came as she walked into the laboratory. 'Get on with your work.'

Beyus thrust his clip-board across the entrance to prevent Mel trotting after the Rani. 'Don't antagonise her! All she has to do is press a button and every Lakertyan will be exterminated!'

'I could nominate a few candidates for extermination myself!' muttered Mel.

Ignoring the petulant remark, Beyus resumed his preparation of the cabinet.

'Surely the Doctor would not let himself be shut up in there,' Mel thought as she read the label. She longed to see her mentor again . . . but not through the glass of one of these tombs . . .

A change of much greater import, at least in the Doctor's opinion, was monopolising his deliberations.

From an underground silo, a sleek, snub-nosed rocket had been jacked up the ramp that cleaved the pyramidal roof of the laboratory complex.

'Mmm, a GTA rocket, sure enough, Ikona.'

Having conducted the Doctor to the vantage point from which they could survey the complex, Ikona regarded this latest, sinister development with dismay.

'Did you notice it's got a fixed trajectory?' asked the Doctor.

'No doubt it'll still play havoc with our planet!'

'Maybe as a side-effect, Ikona. Not the intention.' He craned up at the dark asteroid starkly delineated against the cerise sky. 'I'd say the target is the asteroid of Strange Matter . . . which means the launch is locked in to a precise time.'

'Could it be the Solstice?' The Solstice would be when the asteroid was furthest from Lakertya's equator and nearest to the laboratory complex.

'That's due,' Ikona continued.

'Assuming it is . . . the Rani's overriding priority will be to meet the countdown. No more setbacks or delays . . . I must get into the sealed chamber!'

Recollecting what he had seen of the interior layout, he felt certain the key would be in there. The pulse beat heard through the improvised stethoscope came to mind.

He shuddered. 'That'll be out of the frying pan into the mire!'

'I'll come with you.'

'No.'

'I want to help.'

'You can. By drawing off the guard.'

'That bluff worked once. The Tetraps may not fall for it again.'

'I don't see why not. Start the diversionary tactics, Ikona,' the Doctor ordered, sounding much more optimistic than he felt . . .

The elliptical quadview of the patrolling guard homed in on Ikona. Quitting his post, he gave chase.

Certain the ruse had succeeded, the Doctor scurried into the complex.

A Tetrap eased from a concealed position to block his path!

He spun about: Urak cut off his line of retreat! Yet again the Doctor had been hoodwinked by the Machiavellian Tetrap!

Exposing his teeth in a malevolent grin, Urak closed on the Time Lord. 'We have been . . . expecting you . . . Doctor . . .' The forked tongue flicked the Doctor's cheek . . .

16

The Twelfth Genius

'We must be able to something!' Mel whispered, furtively examining the cabinet ordained for the Doctor. 'Can't we make it blow a fuse?'

'What good would that do?' scolded Beyus. 'At least he'll be kept alive in there.'

'Don't try to reason me into compliance! You're wasting your breath –'

The door to the long, narrow catacomb clattered open.

Urak and the Tetrap guard humped the unconscious Doctor into the sombre arcade.

'No!' screeched Mel as the lumbering brutes dumped the Time Lord into the cabinet. 'Leave him alone!'

She was prevented from hurling herself into an attack by Beyus.

'You . . ! Lakertyan . . !' grunted Urak. 'Connect this . . . specimen to . . . the main input . . .'

'I won't let you!' bawled Mel, struggling to break from Beyus's grip. But the tall, spare Lakertyan leader was too strong. .

'Listen to me!' He shook Mel roughly, then looked defiantly at Urak. 'These Tetraps are competely without conscience. They will not hesitate to kill!'

A sadistic grin split the vulpine face: Urak took the remark as a compliment. He lowered the glass front, sealing the Doctor into the cabinet. 'Set the . . . temperature . . . gauge . . .'

'We're setting nothing!'

'Your stubbornness will not help your friend,' cajoled Beyus as he released her.

'And putting him in there will? That's some twisted philosophy if you like!'

The fight had not gone completely out of Mel but discretion began to oust suicidal valour.

'How far have you got?' The incisive question heralded the Rani's arrival.

'I need to realign the final calibrations before he can be connected to the main input,' stalled Beyus.

'Make certain those levels are kept stable.'

'If you're hoping for any positive results, you're going to be disappointed,' forecast Mel. 'The Doctor won't collaborate.'

'I'm sure – were he able – he'd express his appreciation of such unstinted confidence.' The Rani's amused gaze was on the Doctor who lay with his hat on his knees and his neck clamped into a polyethylene collar from which sprouted the tubes that linked him to the pyramid machines in the laboratory.

'As soon as the activity indicator reaches eight-point-one-five, increase the stimulation,' commanded the Rani.

Not only were the Rani and Beyus absorbed in the task, but the Tetraps also gave it their undivided attention.

Nerves tingling, Mel slipped into the laboratory. Somehow, some way, she had to spike the grisly exercise.

The four pyramids, in full spate, were a lure.

But Mel could not forget the Doctor's obsessive certainty that inside the spherical chamber was the kernel, the nub, of this grandiose scheme.

She tapped nine-five-three into the combination lock.

The panel stayed shut.

She didn't give up.

Five-nine-three.

Again no luck.

Perhaps three-nine-five.

A slender, manicured finger interposed and tapped in the correct code.

The panel glided open.

'Is this what you're looking for?' asked the Rani.

Magenta light washed over Mel. It oscillated rhythmically with an oppressive throbbing from the interior.

Also from within the chamber came a weird, guttural, synthesized voice:

'TO REPRODUCE THE LEPTONIC ERA TEMPERATURE OF TEN TO THE POWER OF TWELVE K, IT WILL BE ESSENTIAL TO CREATE A CATACLYSMIC EXPLOSION THE EQUIVALENT OF A SUPERNOVA.'

Cold tremors trickled down Mel's spine.

Tentatively she went into the spherical chamber . . .

A circular, wrought-iron gantry surmounted by a golden railing caged a massive brain.

Three metres high, composed of a mottled grey and magenta material identical to the liquid in the crystal pyramid tank, the cerebral mass dominated the spherical chamber.

Tiny veins and capillaries ran, like purple rivers, through furrows and grooves, causing the fibrous cells to pulsate with the fluctuating purple glow.

Dumbfounded by the prodigious spectacle, Mel falteringly ventured further in.

Beyond the vibrant brain, dimly lit by the alternating magenta, was the breech of a rocket launcher.

'*WHILE TIME DILATION IS NOT QUES-TIONED . . .*'

Mel jumped: she was alongside the voice syn-thesiser.

'*. . . OUR UNDERSTANDING OF TIME IS STILL AT A PRIMITIVE STAGE.*'

'It won't be when the Doctor adds his contribution!' said the Rani. 'Urak! Bring her to the arcade!'

Urak, even more gruesome in the magenta glow, bundled Mel out and followed the Rani across the laboratory to the arcade.

'Beyus!'

'Yes?'

'Is the Doctor connected to the main input?'

Beyus, making the final adjustments, did not re-spond. In vivid contrast with the intense emotions being generated by the prospect of his contributing to the gigantic brain, the usually hyperactive seventh Doctor reposed in a state of vulnerable serenity.

'I said, is he connected!' rapped the Rani.

'Yes,' replied Beyus reluctantly. 'Everything is ready.'

'No, Beyus! For once don't do as she tells you –' Urak's claw muffled Mel's mouth.

From behind, he crushed her into his downy arms . . . the darting, forked tongue almost licking her ear . . .

'Switch on!'

Beyus obeyed.

A spasm shook the Doctor: the impulses from his brain were ready to be tapped.

'His well-being is in your hands now,' the Rani rasped to Mel. 'Remember that.' She returned into the lab.

Urak drooled as he contemplated the lobe of Mel's

102

ear before pitching her to Beyus's feet.

'You . . . Lakertyan . . . you will be . . . responsible . . . for this creature's . . . behaviour . . .'

Stumbling to her knees, Mel could only stare numbly at the Doctor's cabinet . . .

17

Selective Retribution

On the laboratory monitor screen, the encrusted, gnarled asteroid of Strange Matter could be seen casting its shadow over the planet of Lakertya.

'Time is getting . . . very short if . . . we are to be . . . ready for the . . . Solstice, Mistress . . .'

'I'm aware of that.'

While awaiting the Doctor's unique contribution to augment that of her kidnapped geniuses, the Rani was relaying indices of the satellite's position, weight and velocity into the computer.

'The Doctor must . . . have had help . . .'

'Urak, if you have a point, make it!'

'The culprits could . . . still interfere . . . They should be . . . punished . . .'

The Rani paused. Urak had a point and it was relevant.

'Shall we release . . . the insects in . . . the globe and . . . rid ourselves . . . of all the . . . Lakertyans . . ?'

'Too drastic.'

'It is unchar . . . acteristic . . . of the Mistress . . . to be senti . . . mental . . .'

'Sentiment doesn't come into it. Squandering a resource does. Until this experiment is successfully concluded, I can't be certain I won't need them as a labour force.' From a cupboard in the bench, she extracted a casket of silver bangles. 'Selective retribution will bring any dissidents into line.'

Gleefully, Urak accepted the casket.

The glee rippled contagiously through the eyrie. Their membraned capes fanning the steamy fug, the hanging Tetraps came awake and flopped ecstatically from the rafters.

Not even the pungent ambrosia of the plasma trough enticed them from rallying to Urak's expedition of repression.

Spring-heeled, the ebullient Tetraps stomped from the eyrie, their ungainly progress reflected with clockwork precision in the glass-fronted cabinets.

Mel almost envied the somnolent intellectuals as she fought the surge of nausea evoked by the revolting creatures.

Mental bile sickened Beyus. Watching the Tetraps' departure, he suspected their assignation would bode no good for his subjects.

A paradox. By temperament poles apart from Beyus, the abrasive Ikona was about to experience the same foreboding.

The suspicious ease with which he had evaded the decoyed Tetrap guarding the perimeter, made him ultra-cautious in his return to the environs of the complex.

He was snaking, Indian-fashion, along the ground when the regular beat of marching feet sent him slithering into a rift.

A squad of sinewy, hairy legs stomped past: a tattoo of sound and shadow.

Their destination was the Centre of Leisure.

Storm-trooper style, they clomped down the staircase and raided cubicle after cubicle. The occupants were indiscriminately hauled onto the plaza where a silver, bejewelled bangle was strapped to each timorous Lakertyan's ankle.

106

Urak, cuspids bared and forked tongue darting, oversaw the operation from the gallery.

'Why are you doing this?' Faroon demurred. 'We have co-operated.'

'Silence, Lakert . . . yan! There have . . . been too many . . . unfriendly acts . . .'

'Not by us,' she protested. 'This is unjust.'

The garnet brooch pinned to her apricot cloak was a symbol of her status in Lakertyan society. It did not, however, exempt her from rough treatment.

She was dragged to the fore to receive the unwanted ornament.

'At least tell us what these are for.'

Faroon did not lack courage, but challenging Urak was a maladroit gesture.

'I will demon . . . strate with great . . . enjoyment . . .' His quadview roamed over the servile pleasure seekers.

'You!' he cackled.

His choice was a young female.

'Come forward . . .'

She froze, too scared to move.

Her fear amused Urak.

With a theatrical flourish, he depressed a tab on a facsimile of the Rani's mini-computer-bracelet which he wore, incongruously, on his hairy wrist.

The jewel in the silver bangle on the young female lit up.

A radiant heat spread from her thin, delicate ankle. A heat so intense that her hand, dipping into the pool as she collapsed, caused a cloud of steam to rise from the water.

For a brief, morbid moment, a skeletal fretwork of bones glowed through the flesh. Then, as the heat evaporated, the X-ray image faded . . .

A living being had become a corpse.

18

Too Many Cooks

'The Rani might think she's harnessed the brain of a Time Lord, but she's reckoned without one thing.'

'What's that?' Beyus, yoking and loading buckets of plasma, looked at the slight and defiant Earthling.

'The Doctor's character,' declared Mel fervently.

Almost imperceptibly the entombed Doctor's lips began to move . . . a twitch developed in his cheek . . .

Activity in the crystal tank increased. The Doctor's input mingled with the orderly impulses from the other contributors.

The first sign that Mel may be right, had a mildly absurd manifestation – the goo burped!

Quite distinctly.

The noise penetrated the Rani's cocoon of single-minded concentration.

Tiny lights winked from every instrument indicator on the pyramidal computers.

Again the goo burped.

Not to be outdone, the catalyst gave a particularly loud crack.

Perturbed, the Rani attempted to stem the rising tide of energy by adjusting the regulators.

To no avail. The process was gathering into hectic pace.

'THE BARRIER TO UNDERSTANDING TIME IS EMPIRICAL THINKING. I SUGGEST A LATERAL APPROACH.'

The bland, synthesised voice had taken on a scornful note.

Urgently, the Rani hurried into the spherical chamber.

The furrowed brain appeared about to burst its blood vessels, and a sheath of nerves linking it to the voice box was all of a quiver.

Other synthesised voices joined in.

'*I STILL ASSERT ELECTRON POSITRON PAIRS CAN BE PREVENTED FROM RE-COMBINING INTO PHOTONS.*'

'*REALLY! THIS IS NOT THE PLACE FOR DOUBLE ENTENDRES!*' Could it be the Doctor speaking?

'*YOU ARE ALL CONTRIBUTING GIB-BERISH!*'

'*MY THEORY WILL PROVIDE THE FORMULA.*'

'*A FOOL AND HIS FORMULA ARE SOON PARTED.*' This *had* to be the Doctor!

'*OUTRAGEOUS POLEMICS! GOD DOES NOT PLAY WITH DICE!*' This surely was Einstein!

'*DON'T TELL GOD WHAT TO DO!*' So Niels Bohr, Einstein's rival, was also one of the captive geniuses!

'*GENTLEMEN, SUCH HOSTILITY! RE-MEMBER, BLESSED ARE THE PIEMAKERS FOR THEY SHALL MAKE LIGHT PASTRY.*'

Assailed by the manic babble, the Rani gripped the gantry rail and gaped.

The massive brain, ominously emitting a deepening magenta, was throbbing: a seizure seemed imminent!

'*IT IS A FUNDAMENTAL POSTULATE,*' continued a synthesised voice.

'*THAT ALL MOTION IS RELATIVE.*'

'*YOU WOULDN'T SAY THAT IF YOU'D MET*

MY UNCLE!'

'DISMISSING OPPOSITION AS DECADENT HERESY IS THE REFUGE OF THE REACTIONARY.'

'AH WELL, EVERY DOGMA HAS ITS DAY!'

'PERHAPS WE SHOULD ALL TAKE A SABBATICAL.'

'OR A NUMBER THREE BUS!'

Great slurps and burps of volcanic proportions belched from the crystal tank.

The catalyst cracked like a demented howitzer.

Signal lights blinked and flashed in irrational discord from the overheating pyramids.

Pursued by the bedlam of debate, the Rani made for the arcade.

'I DENY THE UNCERTAINTY PRINCIPLE IS INCOMPATIBLE WITH THE THERMODYNAMICALLY IRREVERSIBLE PROCESS!'

'THE UNCERTAINTY PRINCIPLE IS A SUPERSTITION OF THE SCIENTIFICALLY INEPT.'

'OH – INDUBITABLY – ER – I THINK.'

'THE HYPOTHESIS THAT NEGATIVE GRAVITATIONAL MASS WILL PRODUCE TIME REVERSAL, IS UNTUTORED SPECULATION.'

'I HAVE PROVED CONCLUSIVELY THAT THE RELATIVISTIC SHIFT FOR THE STAR B-SIRIUS IS OVER THIRTY TIMES THAT EXPECTED.'

'I'D SAY YOU'RE LOOKING BACK IN RETROSPECT!'

'IT IS STATED IN THE SPECIAL THEORY AND HAS BEEN DEMONSTRATED, THAT AN INCREASE IN VELOCITY WILL INCREASE

MASS.'
'DOES THAT MEAN, THE FASTER A FAT
MAN RUNS, THE FATTER HE WILL GET?'

'I'll kill him!'

Abdicating any pretence of composure, the Rani ran into the arcade.

Every cabinet was steamed up!

Some rattled as their occupants experienced spasms of agitation.

Frenetically, she disconnected the Doctor . . . and the commotion began to subside.

'The idiot provoked multiple schizophrenia!' she muttered, checking to ensure the eleven other geniuses had suffered no permanent damage.

'Congratulations,' said Mel. 'You brought us here.'

'And I can dispose of you!'

Trembling with rage, she delved into her pocket for a phial. 'This will rid me of a pair of pests –'

The door of the Doctor's cabinet flipped open!

Unseen by her, he had inserted the penknife into the latch and lifted it!

He sprang out – and grabbed the Rani. 'Quickly, Mel! Don't just stand there!'

The suddenness of his attack caused the phial to be jolted from the Rani's grasp.

'Catch it, Mel!'

She turned . . . fumbled . . . and the phial fell to the floor!

But did not break.

Relief immobilised Mel.

'Let go of me, you interfering maniac!' screeched the Rani.

'Mel! Help me!'

Together they stuffed the squirming Rani into the recently occupied cabinet!

'You'll pay for this with your –'

The door slammed shut, cutting off the threat.

'Switch on. Give her a taste of her own medicine,' Mel advised.

'Two wrongs don't make a left turn –'

He gulped.

Brandishing a net-gun, a Tetrap guard had entered the arcade!

Gallantly the Doctor shielded Mel as the Tetrap advanced to investigate the thumps coming from the cabinet.

'Er –' the Doctor politely doffed his hat. 'She's just testing. Um – for a design fault.'

They were cornered. The stalking brute and its net-gun were between them and all avenues to freedom. A brittle snap! The Tetrap had trodden on the phial.

Luminous green fungus coated the hairy foot.

The contamination spread swiftly over its haunches and torso. The Rani's concoction from the phial interbred with the oily skin's abundant microbes and bloomed into spontaneous fungal growth that smothered its victim, infiltrating mouth and nostrils to block the trachea and lungs.

With strangled gasps, the Tetrap slumped to the floor . . .

'She meant that for us,' cried an indignant Mel.

'Yes, well, let's postpone the post-mortem.'

Giving the lichen-shrouded corpse a wide berth, the Doctor picked up the net-gun and tucked it beside a cabinet. 'Waste net want net!'

19

Star Struck!

Self-recrimination scourged Ikona as he watched Urak and the Tetraps emerge boisterously from the Centre of Leisure.

Despite taking a short cut, Ikona had not been able to warn his compatriots of the impending invasion. That his forebodings were well-founded, he had no doubts. The exuberant cavorting and splashing of the loutish creatures traversing the brook, were all the confirmation needed.

Grandly, Urak distributed silver bangles among the troop. '*Naf tuo . . . uoy era erawa . . . fo eht stnuah eseht . . . elbacipsed . . . snaytrekaL . . . tneuqerf . . .*' (By simply reversing the Tetrapyriarban language, this would read: 'Fan out . . . you are aware . . . of the haunts these . . . despicable . . . Lakertyans . . . frequent.')

Braying the equivalent of Tetrapian tally-hos, the winged bipeds rombed cumbersomely into the hunt.

But without their leader. His own malice assuaged, Urak set off for the laboratory complex.

Bracing himself to expect the worst, Ikona went into the Centre of Leisure.

Crestfallen and downcast, mourning Lakertyans presented a tableau of grief.

Averting his gaze from the slain female, Ikona looked to where Faroon was consoling Aragon, an elderly sage who fiddled with a too-tight bangle.

'Don't touch it, Aragon,' Faroon counselled, massaging his leg to ease the pain.

'How much longer must we endure this humiliation?' he quavered.

'As long as Beyus instructs us to . . .'

Ikona did not try to capitalise on Faroon's lack of conviction. A call to mutiny would be an invitation to suicide. Any hopes of salvation now had to be vested in that unpredictable knight errant in a panama hat – the Doctor.

'Once more into the breach!' The misquoting Time Lord poked his head into the rocket launcher's breech.

Despite Mel's entreaties to get clear, he had trotted directly for the spherical chamber.

'I told Ikona this had a fixed trajectory. If I'm right, I can guess the target.'

'Before this regeneration you were keen on cats. And you know what curiosity did to them!'

'I should leave the quotes to the expert,' advised the Doctor, designating himself the expert!

'Fixed trajectory, sure enough,' he said, pulling his head clear of the breech.

'It isn't all that'll be fixed if we don't get out of here!'

The Doctor rested his elbows on the rail circling the mammoth brain. The purple rivulets trickled more sluggishly than when he was on stream, and the sheath of nerves quivered only occasionally.

His abstracted air belied the inner dialogue that saddened him. During his many existences, and on his wanderings through Time and Space, he had seen wonders that filled him with awe. Now, perhaps, he was in audience with the most spectacular of all.

His own brain, like that of every Time Lord, was the ultimate refinement of cosmic evolution. Yet the pulsating reproduction devised by the Rani was a thousandfold greater.

As always, his sadness came from the conviction that her superb ingenuity would add to, rather than alleviate, suffering.

'The Rani's pillaged the universe for the most creative geniuses,' he mused, tipping his hat off his forehead. 'Original thinkers who are capable of making the leap in the dark. Why? Why?'

'Well, she's not infallible,' retorted Mel. 'She made the mistake of trying to use you!'

'You're missing the point.' His irascibility was an expression of self-inadequacy. In quick, fussed movements, he explored a mechanism that comprised a hopper and a crucible.

'Then share the secret. Enlighten me,' taunted Mel.

'Trying to use me was a desperate gamble. So why take it?'

'Conceit,' concluded Mel. 'Blind vanity.'

'Wrong. Don't underestimate her. That could be fatal.'

'Well – oh, I don't know. She was pressed for time.'

'Exactly! I'm sure this planet's solstice is the deadline. And I'm positive that asteroid is the target.'

A bossed beading extruding from the wall had been intriguing him. 'Hmmm – he who dares, spins!'

He spun the beading.

A three-dimensional hologram materialised, dwarfing both them and the corpulent brain.

The dominant element was a colossal star: a sun that burned with spurting gushes of fire spiking from its surface.

Then, a subtle change. A white dot on the fiery surface spread malignantly.

'A supernova . . .' The Doctor was aghast.

In a searing flash that blanched everything in the

117

spherical chamber, the star exploded . . .

Fretful kicks and thumps spasmodically rattled the Rani's cabinet.

They penetrated to Beyus as he emerged from the eyrie.

Warily, he avoided the fungus-infested Tetrap corpse.

'Beyus! Is that you, Beyus?'

Perplexed, he hesitated.

'Get me out of here!' The Rani's features were distorted as she pressed them against the glass.

'Do you hear me? Open this door!'

No response.

'Beyus . . . if you place any value on your people's lives . . . you'll release me!'

The ultimatum left Beyus in an agony of indecision.

'Do you realise how close the Rani must have taken her TARDIS in recording this, Mel?'

In the hologram, the star had been reduced to a molten lump: a miniature of its former size.

'All I realise is we've just seen what she intends to happen to Lakertya! Can she do it, Doctor?'

'Not by my reckoning. The only known detonator for exploding Strange Matter is Strange Matter itself.'

'But you said Strange Matter is incredibly heavy.'

'A chunk the size of a cubic metre – say, a large suitcase – would weigh as much as your Earth.'

He inspected a sheaf of vertical transparent tubes suspended above the crucible. Each tube contained different coloured granules.

'Could she be using the brain to come up with a formula?' Mel speculated.

'. . . for a lightweight substitute? Might explain why she needs a crucible.' His prowling continued, his unease increased.

'Then – haven't we found the answer?'

'Not completely, Mel. What I can't fathom' – he pointed to the dead star – 'is why the Rani took such an incredible risk to record a supernova.'

'To discover how to reconstruct the same event?'

'More than that. She wouldn't simply be interested in a display of pyrotechnics. Too negative.' He was truly baffled. 'She'd have a deeper motive.' He jabbed a forefinger into each temple. 'The answer's in here!'

'Calm down, Doctor. Let's apply a bit of logic, shall we? What is it you can contribute that those other geniuses can't?'

'A knowledge of time! Oh, a great discovery!' He jigged about the circular gantry, his correspondent shoes rattling on the grids. 'I'd worked that out ages ago!'

The clatter of footsteps.

Mel peeked into the lab.

'The Rani!'

20

Holy Grail

For Mel, survival expunged all other considerations. She scooted into a recess separating the crucible from the rocket's breech.

Flustered, the Doctor was torn between the same instinct and the paramount need to uncover what the Rani hoped to achieve by her extraordinary efforts.

He remained still.

'So now you know.' The Rani regarded the Doctor with calculated sangfroid.

'Not the full story. The last chapter's missing.' Anxious to divert her from discovering Mel, he indicated the magenta brain. 'Keeping quiet, isn't it?'

'Perhaps, unlike you, it speaks only when it's got something intelligent to say.' Gradually she shifted her position in her quest for Mel.

'Possibly,' replied the Doctor. 'On the other hand, it could be wondering why you want Helium Two . . .'

The Rani halted. Temporarily thrown.

'That is why you're seeking to explode Strange Matter, isn't it? To re-enact the Leptonic Era and so secure Helium Two?'

The Leptonic Era to which the Doctor was referring was a microsecond period after the Big Bang that gave birth to the Universe: a moment of mind-boggling temperatures which, if marginally protracted, would have produced the fabulous substance, Helium Two.

'If only you didn't choose to waste your talents on

superficial exploits, you could be quite brilliant, Doctor.'

'I'd never be as scientifically brilliant as you, Rani.'

'Flattery? Too obvious a ploy.' She was abreast of the crucible and nearer to Mel . . .

'Not flattery. I deliberately said scientific brilliance. When it comes to the less attractive aspects of your nature, you're congenitally unbalanced.'

'You could have it wrong. What you call balance could be chaos.'

'Well, that's the way of the world and nothing can change it.' The pat cliché was merely a subterfuge. He was trying to determine why the Rani was humouring him. Perhaps she wasn't beyond redemption. At university, in their debates, they had enjoyed many an academic battle of wits. She'd even confessed to a grudging admiration of his own versatility. A whiff of nostalgia maybe? Plus, as Mel had suggested earlier, a smidgen of vanity.

How wrong these assumptions were.

When Beyus released her from the cabinet, the Rani had seen the dead Tetrap guard. Until Urak returned, she alone had to hold the fort!

'Nothing can change it? I think I can negate that fallacy.' She tossed her head. Her scarlet earrings, looking like scarlet droplets of blood, swirled against her brunette tresses. 'The last chapter, Doctor? The dénouement?'

She spun the bossed beading and the planet of Lakertya replaced the spent star in the hologram. 'In the aftermath of the Strange Matter explosion, Helium Two will fuse with the upper zones of the Lakertyan atmosphere to form a shell of chronons.'

In concert with the dissertation, an explosion engulfed the cerise gases enveloping Lakertya. When it subsided, a shimmering shell had crystallised.

'I don't have to tell you what chronons are, Doctor.'

'Indeed you don't. Discrete particles of time.'

'In the same millisecond the chronon shell is being formed, the hothouse effect of the gamma rays will cause the primate cortex of this brain to go into chain reaction.' A further spin of the beading. 'Multiplying until the gap between shell and planet is filled.'

In the hologram, the gap between the chronon shell and Lakertya's surface was filling with the primate cortex – the segment of the brain responsible for thought.

A shock of realisation ravaged the Doctor: there was to be an immense conjugation of time particles and the brain cells distilled from the intellectual giants.

'You're going to – turn this planet . . . into a Time Manipulator,' he stammered.

'A cerebral mass capable of dominating and controlling time anywhere in the cosmos!'

Mel had been forgotten by the two Gallifreyans. But the enormity of the revelations reduced her own concern for survival to an irrelevance.

The obscenity of the proposition had even robbed the Doctor of speech.

'All I need to bring it about,' continued the Rani, 'is the material for exploding Strange Matter. And my congress of geniuses here' – lovingly she stroked the railing surrounding the brain – 'will provide me with the means of obtaining that.'

'I've underestimated you.' The Doctor's voice was hoarse with disgust. 'I thought science had blinded you. But it's power.'

'Wrong again.'

'They should never have banished you from Gallifrey. They should have locked you in a padded cell!' It was a sentiment the Doctor had given vent to before.

'If the Time Lords hadn't refused to intervene in the pedestrian evolution of other species, a Time Manipulator wouldn't be necessary!'

Cheeks flushed in the magenta glow, she strolled the circular gantry.

'I still can't believe – a Time Manip –' The Doctor was struggling to marshal his thoughts. 'This – this monstrosity will give you . . . the ability to . . . change the order of Creation!'

'Creation's chaotic. I'll *introduce* order. An order based on logic not the capricious whims of chance.'

She switched off the hologram.

'Wherever evolution has taken the wrong route, I'll redirect it.'

'Redirect . . .' repeated the Doctor, staring at his arrogant antagonist.

'That planet you're so obsessed with – Earth – I shall return to the Cretaceous Age. The potential of the dinosaurs was never fully exploited.'

'Cretaceous Age . . .' Mel mouthed in silent horror.

'Shakespeare . . . Louis Pasteur . . . Michelangelo . . . Elvis . . . Even Mrs Malaprop . . . will never have existed!' The Doctor gasped.

Mel, however, was not the sole eavesdropper. Urak had returned to the laboratory.

'Your concern with those minions on Earth is pathetic,' said the Rani. 'They're an inferior species.'

Instead of putting himself at his Mistress's disposal, Urak remained by the laboratory exit, listening.

'To be cast into oblivion?'

'Why not?'

'The same with Lakertya? All life on this planet would become extinct?'

'An unfortunate side-effect.'

'Every living creature left behind – will be ex-terminated?'

'Of which you will be one, Doctor.'

Urak's jaws widened in a grin. He squatted on his haunches, enjoying the obsequies emanating from the spherical chamber.

'There'll be no pain,' continued the Rani. 'In microseconds Lakertyans will be reduced to dust.'

'While you float off safely in your TARDIS.'

'Oh, I shall be back. Once the turbulence has passed.'

'I believed you were a psychopath without murderous intent. I withdraw that qualification –'

'*EIGHTY-SEVEN TO THE POWER OF NINE-TEEN E –*' interrupted the synthesised voice.

Throbbing undulations rippled the purple furrows and grooves of the gestating brain.

'*– CORRELATED WITH FIFTY-TWO TO THE POWER OF SIX-POINT-FOUR EQUALS TWENTY-NINE V –*'

'Thirty-nine! The Doctor's correction was automatic. 'Er – I mean, twenty-nine – yes, yes, twenty!' Too late did he realise he had aided the brain in making the crucial breakthrough.

'*CORRECTION IS NOTED,*' intoned the synthesised voice.

'*THIRTY-NINE TO THE POWER OF V PLUS W . . . EUREKA! OBJECTIVE ACHIEVED!*'

Simultaneously there came the rising sonic whine of a power unit. The coloured granules in the sheaf of transparent tubes began to cavort and dance.

Then the sheaf rotated . . . gathering momentum . . . until it became a variegated blur.

Abruptly, the high-pitched screech became muted . . . beneath the centrifuge, a globule of glistening, phosphorescent alloy took shape.

'*LOYHARGIL!*' pronounced the synthesised voice.

'I knew it! I knew they could do it!' Elated, everything but the triumphant achievement effaced, the Rani went to the crucible to pay homage to the miracle of Loyhargil.

Just the opportunity the Doctor needed.

Signalling to Mel, he slipped from the spherical chamber – and into more trouble!

21

A Dangerous Break

Once Mel was safely in the lab, the Doctor slapped the locking mechanism and the panel slid, shutting the Rani inside the spherical chamber.

They dashed for the exit, where Fate dealt them an unkind blow – Urak blocked it!

'The arcade!'

Fleet-footed, Mel was in the van of the helter-skelter retreat.

Urak hesitated, undecided whether to release the Rani or chase after the absconders. He opted for the latter and trundled towards the arcade.

Once in the arcade, Urak exhibited no hesitation. He turned in the direction that led to the outside. Where else would the craven pair of troublemakers have gone?

Not a very astute conclusion. Limited though his acquaintance with the Doctor was, Urak should have known the obvious rarely appealed to the eccentric Time Lord.

His Tetrapian rearview eye registered the mistake the instant the net-gun fired . . . and it was with a bellow of rage Urak crumpled beneath the mesh of sparks.

The Doctor, his memory revving in overdrive, had remembered the net-gun he had propped beside a cabinet when the Tetrap guard was despatched by the Rani's fungal concoction. He had steered Mel towards the eyrie and lain in wait. The gamble succeeded: Urak was effectively neutralised!

'Get clear of the danger zone, Mel! I'll catch you up.' This order was barked with such authority that Mel was haring across the grounds before her propensity to question the Doctor's wisdom re-asserted itself.

However, back-tracking was pre-empted. An ally, in the shape of Ikona, beckoned.

In a whirl of windmilling limbs, wrenching open cupboards and drawers, the Doctor searched the laboratory.

'Ah! That's the wicket!' he exclaimed, extracting a flask with a rocco stopper. Pocketing it, he spotted his furled umbrella lying beside the bench. Claiming that too, he raised his hat to the spherical panel in a saucy adieu to the imprisoned Rani – and scarpered!

Coming from the plasma bank, Beyus flinched. The arcade resembled a graveyard. One Tetrap was a fungus-barnacled corpse, and another was lying beneath a net.

He lifted the corner of the net . . . Urak's veiny eyelids fluttered.

The only movement in the Centre of Leisure was from the fountains spewing their jets of water into the pool.

'You are sure of this, Doctor?' called Faroon, when the Doctor finished speaking from the gallery.

'Every word I've spoken is the truth, Faroon.'

Although declamatory oration from elevated positions was anathema to him, the Doctor, yielding to Ikona's and Mel's browbeating, had delivered a resumé of the Rani's intent to the Lakertyans assembled below.

'And you are certain she can do it?'

'She has the means. The Loyhargil was all she needed.'

'Faroon,' intervened Mel ardently, 'you've got two choices. Sit tight and wait for the Rani to load that Loyhargil into the rocket and blow up the asteroid. Or try to stop her. Believe me, reducing every Lakertyan to dust is an unimportant side-effect in her book!'

'A precise précis of what I've just said,' agreed the Doctor.

'And for pity's sake stir yourselves!' Ikona castigated the throng in the plaza. 'The Solstice is almost upon us! Either your take action now, or you perish!'

Molten Loyhargil poured into the mould.

Tinted by the magenta light of the spherical chamber, the Rani's face was animated with excitement.

Urak, grudgingly released by Beyus, had unlocked the panel. Still debilitated, he was propped against the wall.

'The Doctor should . . . be apprehen . . . ded . . .'

'He's irrelevant. I have the Loyhargil. Nothing can stop me now!'

A cloud of steam spumed as the mould was dunked into a tub of coolant.

'Unless you tell us how to remove these, we can't help you.' Faroon's conversion was achieved but the bangles were a lethal inhibition.

'Hmmm,' mused the Doctor, examining Faroon's bangle. 'You've got to give the Rani full marks for ingenuity.'

'Maybe if we're careful, we can cut them?' suggested Ikona.

'That's a daft idea!' This could only be Mel! 'They're bound to be booby-trapped!'

129

'Less of the pessimism, Mel.' The Doctor was delicately prodding the jewel with his penknife. 'Not all the cards are in the Rani's flavour. Ah!' He prised off the jewel exposing a micro-circuit. 'If we could loop an extension wire from here to here' – indicating the two minute terminals – 'the circuit wouldn't be broken when the bangle was opened. Mel?'

'Yes?'

'You're the computer expert. How about it?'

'Where am I going to get the right kind of wire?'

Tearing a video game from its moorings, Ikona ripped the power pack from its innards and dumped it in Mel's lap.

'Where there's a will, there's a . . .' he faltered.

'A beneficiary!' chortled the Doctor.

Mel peeled a length of wire from a co-axial lead.

'Hold your horses! I can't guarantee this is going to work!'

Betraying none of the trepidation she felt, Faroon thrust her ankle forward for the experiment.

Smoothing the wrinkled wire, Mel inserted it into the terminals with unerring accuracy.

'Faroon, if I'm wrong about this . . .'

'Go ahead.'

Taking a deep breath, Mel unhooked the clip fastening the bangle . . .

The bypass worked!

'Splendid. Don't know what you were worrying about,' blustered the Doctor, giving Mel a congratulatory tilt of his hat. 'Necessity's mother laughs at locksmiths.'

'Love!' corrected Mel. 'And invention!'

'What's that got to do with it?'

'Necessity is the mother of invention. And love laughs at locksmiths!'

'Er, quite.' The Doctor officiously took charge.

130

'Ikona, you help Mel remove the bangles. Faroon, I'm going to need your assistance in organising the Lakertyans.'

'Haven't you overlooked something, Doctor?' She indicated the revolving globe. 'If the Rani releases the insects in there, we'll all be dead!'

'Then we'll have to finesse her, won't we?'

'Finesse?'

'A double-bluff. Speciality of mine . . .'

Reverentially, the Rani and Urak loaded a slender cartridge, vibrant with potent but latent energy, onto a belt that conveyed it smoothly into the rocket's breech.

With orchestrated dedication, she checked the data feedback comparator. The error detector registered nil and the data from the systems analyser reported that everything was functioning within permitted tolerances.

One further check was necessary.

On the monitor screen, the orbiting asteroid destined to consign history to a nuclear furnace was but a hair's breadth from the superimposed graphic that depicted the point of the Solstice.

'You'll stay here and guard the perimeter until after lift-off, Urak.'

'*After* lift-off . . . Mistress . . ?'

'You said yourself the Doctor could still make trouble. Get out there and see he doesn't.'

'And . . . where will the . . . Mistress be . . ?'

'In my TARDIS. I want to record the experiment from there.'

'I would prefer . . . to be with you . . .'

'Undoubtedly. But you can't!'

She returned to the spherical chamber.

131

No grin split the vulpine nozzle. Instead, beneath the cockscomb of bristle, the pupil in the bloodshot orb dilated as his quadview focused on a single image . . . that of the disappearing Rani, an imperious flounce of scarlet and gold . . .

22

Countdown

Crisply, decisively, the Rani initiated the countdown.

Impersonally, the synthesised voice began to intone the descent to purgatory. Concomitantly, the corresponding numbers clicked over loudly on an automatic digital display.

Experiencing an almost intoxicating exhilaration, the usually unemotional Rani contemplated the spherical chamber. Satisfied, she re-entered the lab.

The drone of the synthesised countdown together with the metronomic clicking, could be clearly heard as the Rani skirted the four pyramid machines and crossed elatedly to the exit.

The solitude of the arcade heightened Beyus's sense of isolation. His certitude had never been absolute despite his public utterances. Now the calamitous misfortune that had befallen Lakertya was reaching its climax, he could not rid himself of the insidious suspicion that his stance, however well-intentioned, was flawed: a *volte-face* so painful Beyus shied away from it, clinging to the hope that his initial premise was correct.

It was a hope that was shattered by the unexpected arrival of Faroon.

'It's clear. Come along, Doctor,' she called, having ensured only Beyus was present.

The Doctor entered.

'You were told not to listen to him!'

Ignoring Beyus's censure, the Doctor eased open the door to the lab. Faintly, the countdown could be heard. 'When that voice reaches zero, there'll be nobody left on Lakertya to listen to me or anyone else!'

'You were warned about his glib tongue!'

'Believe me . . . the Doctor's telling the truth!'

Convincing Beyus was not the Doctor's immediate priority. Leaving Faroon to cope with the task, he went to the portal of the eyrie.

Baulking at going inside, he surreptitiously lowered the grating, shot home the securing bolt, and tiptoed back to the arcade.

'What is it you want me to do?' asked Beyus.

'See who's in the lab.'

Faroon accompanied Beyus while the Doctor nipped to the exit door. 'Coast's clear!'

Ikona and Mel hastened in.

'Right, quickly, all hands to the stumps!'

'Pumps!' corrected Mel, busying herself disconnecting Einstein's cabinet.

Ikona, new to the arcade, joined the Time Lord who was disengaging Louis Pasteur's cabinet.

'Take good care of him, Ikona.'

'He is someone important?' said Ikona, peering with curiosity through the glass.

'Louis Pasteur will rid his world of a major scourge. He'll save the lives of tens of millions.'

'Hey, come on! This isn't a conducted tour!' yelled Mel. 'Don't just stand there gawping, Ikona. We've got to get all of these characters to the TARDIS!'

'You'll deafen them before we get there if you don't stop that squawking!' Bemused he might be, but subdued he was not!

'Doctor, come through,' Faroon urged.

In the spherical chamber, the Doctor put into

motion the first stage of his plan. Willing himself to ignore the relentless countdown, he tampered with the relay loop of the voice synthesiser box.

Then came the next stage.

It involved his trusty umbrella. Not giving a fig for superstition, he opened it indoors.

Strung from the spokes were the silver bangles of death . . .

The eleven bewildered geniuses, some unsteady from their enforced incarceration, were filing from the arcade.

'You know where the TARDIS is, Ikona,' declared Mel. 'We'll meet you there.'

Not waiting for his agreement, she raced to fetch the Doctor.

'Hurry, Doctor! Hurry!' Mel burst into the spherical chamber with but a single thought in mind.

'Mel, there's something bothering me . . .'

'The only thing you've got to worry about is that!' She pointed defiantly at the digital clock. 'We haven't a second to spare!'

'Mel's right,' Beyus said. 'I'll finish in here.'

If the third and crucial stage of his plan was to succeed, the Doctor knew he should accept the exhortations. But there were elements unfolding that he had not anticipated.

'Beyus, don't leave it too late.'

'I know what I have to do.'

'Doctor! Come on!' Mel tugged him into the lab.

'Go with them, Faroon.'

'Can't I wait for you, Beyus?'

'It has not been your habit to question my actions, Faroon. This is not a good moment to begin.'

Reluctantly she complied with his wishes.

135

Positioned so that she could see the rocket, the Rani stood beside her TARDIS.

Ten. Nine. Eight. The countdown was simulated on her mini-computer-bracelet.

'SEVEN . . . SIX . . . FIVE . . .' intoned the synthesised voice in the spherical chamber.

The approaching zero did not rufflle Beyus's calm. He had jammed the umbrella through the interior locking mechanism. This meant neither the Rani nor her loathsome acolyte, Urak, could get in . . . equally it meant he was trapped inside . . .

Beyus had also carried out the Doctor's instructions.

Hooked over the golden rail surrounding the magenta brain, were the bejewelled silver bangles . . .

' . . . FOUR . . . FOUR . . . FOUR . . .'

Four . . . four . . . four . . . ticked on the Rani's mini-computer-bracelet. Frowning, she tapped the dial –

'It's over! You're beaten, Rani!' The Doctor's shout came from some distance away. 'I've aborted the launch. And the Lakertyans are preparing to attack!'

On cue, Lakertyans, male and female, moved from cover. They advanced, their colourful robes easily discernible against the granite grey rocks.

'You imbecile! You've signed their death warrants!' she yelled and viciously stabbed buttons on her computer-bracelet.

In unison, the jewels on the bangles strung to the golden railing, glowed . . . then flashed into the searing white heat of a multiple explosion that consumed the brain and devastated the spherical chamber – exactly as the Doctor had planned.

A homily he was fond of expounding praised the virtues of simplicity: a credo to which he should have adhered. The scheme had been a mite too elaborate. Vibrations from the explosion jolted the voice synthesiser.

'. . . *FOUR . . . THREE . . . TWO . . .*' the countdown had been inadvertently reactivated.

'. . . *ONE . . . LIFT OFF!*'

Smoke snorted from the rocket's take-off boosters!

23

Goodbye, Lakertya

Majestically, the ground-to-air missile rose from the ramp. The downdraughting flames scorched and blackened the pyramidal roof of the complex. Velocity built up, surging through Mach one . . . Mach two . . . until the dynamic rocket, accelerating to escape-speed, thrust through the cerise upper atmosphere.

In curling plumes of smoke, it jettisoned the boosters and angled towards the gnarled asteroid of Strange Matter.

Faces uplifted, taut with strain, Faroon and Mel, Ikona and his scholarly charges, watched for sight of the harbinger of death – a blinding flash of light which would herald the incinerating fireball. There was no comfort in the knowledge that the end, should it come, would be instantaneous.

Breezily, the Doctor joined the forlorn group.

'Not to worry, Mel. The delay in lift-off means the rocket will miss the asteroid.'

'Are you certain?' She was no coward: if the Grim Reaper was about to swing his scythe, Mel didn't want to be fobbed off with a glib bromide.

'Oh, absolutely! A miss is as good as a smile!'

Luckily Mel could not see behind the Time Lord's back – where all eight fingers were crossed!

Exhaust gases burning, the rocket drew nearer to the asteroid. From ground level, it seemed impossible it could miss.

But miss it did.

To become a dwindling nomad hurtling into the infinite void of space.

It was not the only object disappearing into that emptiness.

The Rani's instinctive reaction at being outwitted, was to boil over in frustration and fury. But she was a realist. Lakertya and its asteroid of Strange Matter had become a lost cause.

She retreated into her pyramid TARDIS and, with a bellow like a ruptured elephant, it dematerialised.

The mournful bellow was an appropriate requiem for the Rani's shattered dreams. More than that, amid the ashes of the magenta brain and the scattered debris of equipment, was a tattered orange cloak. In his atonement, Beyus had paid the ultimate price.

Conducted into the Doctor's police box, the geniuses' curiosity overflowed. The relative dimensions of temporal physics was a concept that intrigued them. How could the interior be greater than the exterior?

'Explanations later,' said the Doctor, ushering the motley band into the TARDIS's comfortable lounge.

A promise he meant to keep. But the secrets they were to learn would never be revealed. The Time Lord intended to return them, individually, to the exact situation they had been enjoying when the Rani snatched them – only his delivery would be made a microsecond before the kidnapping.

A microsecond before the adventure began.

An adventure that, for the geniuses, therefore, never happened.

The same consolation was not available to Faroon as

she gazed at Beyus's funeral pyre.

'I'm so sorry, Faroon.' Exiting from the TARDIS, the Doctor, with his intuitive empathy, felt compelled to offer condolences. 'When I think of Beyus, I shall remember with admiration the sacrifice he made.'

'He must have been convinced it was the only way to be certain of saving the rest of us.'

'He'll not be forgotten,' asserted Ikona.

'Nor will you, Doctor,' said Faroon, flattening her right palm against the Doctor's palm in the Lakertyan parting salute.

'Oh, I dare say we'll pop in again some day.'

'You will be most welcome, Doctor.'

'Ready, Mel?'

'Yes . . . Cheerio, Ikona.'

'I wish I were coming with you, Mel . . .'

'Nobody will credit this – least of all you – but so do I . . .' She raised her palm inviting him to bid her farewell according to his custom.

'I do have another regret.'

'What's that, Ikona?' asked the Doctor.

'After all the suffering she's caused, the Rani has escaped, unscathed, in her TARDIS!'

Glancing quizzically heavenwards, the Doctor wondered if that were true. The question nagging him since they attacked the laboratory still hadn't been answered.

Where were the Tetraps?

The noisome, hairy bipeds were hanging from the ceiling of the control room in the Rani's TARDIS. Already their rancid odour was impregnating the clinical furnishings.

Suspended upside-down with them was a slim, writhing, scarlet-clad body.

Competently dealing with the instrumentation on

the console was the grinning Urak: student had graduated to master! His quadview scanning, he padded to the distraught Rani.

'Mistress . . .' With the callousness he had demonstrated when she had lain stunned beneath his electronic net, Urak brushed the dangling brunette tresses from her upside-down features. 'You have taught . . . us so much . . . When we get to . . . Tetrapyri . . . arbus, your . . . incredible . . . brain will show us . . . how we conquer . . . our needs . . . There will be . . . plasma in . . . abundance . . .'

'*Amsalp* . . !' Slimy rodent lips dribbled in anticipation.

Urak's ivory cuspids gleamed. His forked tongue lasciviously pricked the Rani's cheek . . . and as paralysis stiffened every sinew, the Rani's vision was filled with the celebratory flapping of oily, membraned wings and rolling bloodshot eyes . . .

'*Amsalp* . . . *Amsalp* . . .' The Tetrapyriaban cry echoed . . .

'Oh, memory like a dromedary!' About to go into the TARDIS, the Doctor suddenly smacked the top of his hat. Rummaging in his pocket, he extracted the flask with the rococo stopper he had purloined from the lab.

'Antidote for those killer insects in the globe,' he explained, giving the flask to Ikona. 'The Rani always takes out an insurance policy.'

Ikona accepted the flask, removed the stopper – and emptied the contents on the ground!

'You're impossible!' Mel did not expect the iconoclastic Ikona to show gratitude, but this! 'Why did you do that?'

'Tell her, Faroon,' said the young Lakertyan.

'Ikona believes our people must meet their own challenges if they are to survive.'

142

The Doctor did not question the philosophy.

'You know, Mel,' he confided as they turned again to the TARDIS. 'Ikona reminds me of myself when I was his age.'

'*That* I can believe!'

He stood aside for her to enter the TARDIS.

'In you go, Mel. Time and tide melts the snowman.'

'Waits for no man!'

'Who's waiting? I'm ready.'

Mel looked at the mischievous face, the small, wiry frame in its cream coat, flattened straw hat and correspondent shoes. Now the umbrella was destroyed, all outward semblances of the sixth Doctor were lost.

'You're going to take a bit of getting used to,' she groaned.

The final assertion to be heard from the seventh Doctor before the TARDIS dematerialised were the optimistic words:

'Oh, I'll grow on you, Mel. I'll grow on you!'